TURNING A BLIND EYE

A NOVEL

ANTHONY ENGLE

TURNING A BLIND EYE

A NOVEL

TURNING A BLIND EYE

Sweety Tweety Books titles may be ordered from your favorite bookseller.
www.SweetyTweety.com

Sweety Tweety Books
c/o CMI
13518 L. Street
Omaha, NE 68137

Company names, products, services and other brand names used are owned solely by their respective trademark holders and are not endorsements or critiques of any of the brand names used. This is a work of fiction. Any similarities to actual people, events, or places are purely coincidental.

ISBN: 978-1-945505-13-3 (sc)
ISBN: 978-1-945505-14-0 (eBook)

LCCN: 2016910833
Library of Congress cataloging in publication data on file with publisher.

Printed in the USA

10 9 8 7 6 5 4 3 2

INTRODUCTION

This book was developed from one of my dreams in which I was at the vending convention for the blind and spontaneously decided to rob the hotel with my wife and two daughters. We took everything out of the vault and went home to split the contents among us. I have been to some of the places described in the book; other places were described in old-time radio programs. Please be advised that there is strong violence in the contents of this book. I'm writing this manuscript solely for enjoyment and excitement. This is a fictional biography of Frank Zuccini's life, detailing its unrest and drama as he commits crimes and what he plans to do when he finally has to pay for his mistakes. Other characters involved are Frank's family and friends, police, FBI, and the women and men of the courts. Let's travel with Frank as he tells of his adventures and dangerous life.

Hello. My name is Frank Zuccini. I'm five foot four and 185 pounds. I was born in Chicago to Paul and Mary Zuccini. My father is five foot eight and 200 pounds. I got my brown hair and blue eyes from him. Mother is five foot and petite with curly, long brown hair. My brother Paul looks almost identical to our father, being six foot with brown hair and weighing 220 pounds; the only difference is the brown eyes Paul got from Mother. He wears blue jeans and a T shirt, and he lives in Nebraska where he works at a factory. Dorris, my sister, is five foot one with blond hair, blue eyes, and a stature similar to Mother, weighing only 120 pounds.

My childhood was normal; I went bowling, swimming, and to the movies.

My interests include listening to the blues or metal, playing and watching sports, and learning Spanish.

I live in a crowded apartment. The living room is ten by twelve feet with a thirty-two-inch flat screen TV, a desktop computer sitting on a table, and overstuffed furniture.

We will start at my first job as a vending operator at the First National Bank in Chicago. I was recently transferred to Peoria, Illinois, and everything is all right so far. The bank building I work in is old and five stories high, with several offices on the upper floors.

My life is hard. The vending money I'm making is peanuts compared to what I could make by taking things that don't belong to me, so I start out stealing from machines, things such as cigarettes, money from changers, and other items.

My life of crime becomes more intense after I get married to Jacqueline. She is a large woman—five foot five, 285 pounds, with brown hair and brown eyes. Her two daughters are part of the action. Susanne, the youngest, is five foot eight, 250 pounds with brown hair and brown eyes. Peggy is half a foot shorter than her younger sister with blond hair, but the same brown eyes, and weighing 135 pounds.

It's a Saturday night in mid-October. The four of us are at the vending convention together at the Holiday Inn, which is decorated with plants, flowers, and plush carpeting throughout the building.

Jackie says, "We need to talk."

"What's going on?" I ask.

We all huddle together as Jackie talks softly. "We're here to rob the hotel vault."

"What's the plan?" I ask.

Susanne says, "We will have a talk with hotel management and say we have guest valuables that are kept in the vault. They will lead us to the vault where we will grab all we can and hurry back home."

"We'll need a getaway driver." I say. "I'll call Tim."

After Tim, my high school friend, is in on the plan, we get in the elevator, and it takes us to the second floor where the vault is located. As we enter, Peggy is in front, followed by Jackie and Susanne, and I am holding up the rear.

"We have come for valuables; make it quick." Susanne says to Dave, the hotel manager, with a serious look on her face.

The managers are scared and surprised; they unwillingly give us all gifts, jewelry, and cash out of the gigantic vault. We run out as fast as we can as two security guards storm in to prevent the robbery. We hear, "Stop! Don't let them get away!" as my family and I hurry through the screaming crowd and into the elevator. We get off in the main lobby and check out without saying a word.

Sirens are heard part of the way as Tim drives us away in a 1994 mini-van. Tim is five foot ten and 195 pounds with red hair and blue eyes. The stash is to be split evenly among the five of us.

John Schnyder and Steve Davis of the Chicago robbery detail are assigned to the case for investigation.

"Hi. I'm Steve Davis, and this is my partner, John Schnyder," says Steve.

"I'm glad you came. We want these crooks," says Dave with disappointment.

"Can you tell us what happened in detail please?" John asks.

Dave says, "What I remember was that there were two women and two men because one guy had a cane."

"Is there anything else?" asks Steve.

Both officers are dressed in uniform with the badge in front and thirty-eight caliber pistols at their sides. They are both muscular and physically fit, standing about six foot three and weighing 245 pounds.

Dave says, "One lady told us, 'We've come for our valuables.'"

"Yes, sir, what else can you remember?" asks John.

Dave is really shaken up and isn't sure, so he calls for Mike who is also still in shock as he enters the office.

"We're glad to meet you, sir. I'm Steve Davis and this is my partner, John Schnyder."

"Please help us," says Mike with relief on his face.

"Can you remember anything that happened?" asks John.

"I remember that three women and one man entered the vault area."

"My bad; there were three women and one man," Dave announces.

"I remember one of the women told us they had come for valuables and to be quick," says Mike.

John and Steve write on their clipboards and continue.

"Can you describe anyone involved?" asks Steve.

Dave says, "One of the women was average build, two were heavyset, and the man was short, muscular, and he used a cane."

"That's right; he was in back of the line when they made their appearance." Mike adds.

"What about their hair or their eyes? Can you think of anything to add?" asks John.

"No," says Mike.

"Can you recall their height and weight?" Steve asks.

"No," Mike and Dave say.

The phone rings, and Dave picks up the receiver. "Hello can we help you?" He asks.

"We need a room."

"I'm sorry, ma'am, we're busy. Can you call back?" Dave asks politely.

The customer replies, "Sorry I called late. I'll call back."

"I'm sorry for wasting your time." Dave hangs up the phone and hears Steve say, "That's what we're here for, and we'll try to get your stuff back."

ANTHONY ENGLE | 7

Mike says, "The man was part of the blind vendor convention."

John and Steve finish their notes and say, "We thank you for your time, and you've been a big help. Here are our cards, and have a good night. Give us a call at the office if you need anything." John and Steve get up from their chairs, hand their cards to managers, and head to the car.

John asks, "What do you make of this, Steve?"

"It's time to interview everyone involved with the convention and report to Captain Edwards." he answers as they climb into their 2000 Chevy Malibu. They drive back to their office, which is encircled with awards and plaques that were received from their combined thirty years of investigation.

Captain Edwards is in his late fifties, six feet tall with black hair, brown eyes and 195 pounds. He is wearing a gray pinstriped suit with several pins acquired from his veteran status in the military and law enforcement.

"What have we got so far?" Edwards asks with a determined look on his face.

Steve says, "What we have is there were four people involved— three women and one visually impaired man."

"That's right sir." adds John.

💰

Back in Peoria, I'm trying to resume my life as a vendor, but that isn't working out. A meeting is scheduled with the program director and another vendor to represent me. Director Nick Drake is seated to my right. He is wearing a pinstriped suit with the inscription "Dors" on the front, and he stands six foot one with gray hair and blue eyes. He has a serious look of anger on his face. The other vendor to my left is wearing a gray suit and is an African American man who stands five foot seven and weighs 150 pounds; he also has a very serious look.

"We need to talk." says the director.

I'm sitting at the table, shaking with paranoia and depression inside.

"What do we need to talk about?" I ask with a worried voice.

"It's come to my attention that you're stealing from the program."

The other vendor, Larry Jackson, says, "Frank has told me several times that's a lie. He hasn't been stealing anything."

Mr. Drake tries to hand me a piece of paper. "This paper is to let you know that we took inventory to kick you out of the program." says Mr. Drake.

"Whatever. This is bull crap."

Mr. Drake says, "You're lucky that you are not in jail now! Mr. Jackson and I have investigated and found that you've marked invoices paid when none of the suppliers are paid, and there's money stolen from all the machines!"

I apathetically rip up the paper and storm out of the building.

Rick and George are two friends that I met when I used to work at the bank building. They follow me out of the building. George is African American and stands six foot three, weighing 180 pounds. Rick is also an African American who stands five foot eleven and weighs 240 pounds. They have just found out that Jackie, Susanne, and Peggy left for Nebraska and are planning to turn me in to the authorities for the hotel heist.

"Let's go to Tim's house so we can speak in private." George suggests.

We're in Tim's basement, which is a finished room with cheap living room furniture.

"They are in as much trouble as I am." I fume.

Tim says, "We don't know those ladies. What's our next move?"

"You know, we're being watched, so be careful what you say." Rick warns.

Just then, the phone rings. Tim picks up the receiver. "Hello, this is Tim."

"What's going on? We're having a party. Can you come over?" Scott asks on the line.

"Yeah. I've got Frank, Rick, and George with me."

"Sweet, we'll see you there. There's plenty to eat and drink."

Tim hangs up the phone and says, "Scott's a huge man, six foot six and 300 pounds, and he has brown hair and blue eyes. The party is at his place on Springfield Hill in East Peoria."

We pass around a joint and drink a few beers before leaving for the party.

Jackie, Susanne, and Peggy hire an attorney named Travis Fitzpatrick, who is six foot one, weighs 280 pounds, and has blond hair and blue eyes.

"Hi, glad to be with you ladies. How can I be of service?" asks Travis.

"We want to turn ourselves and my husband in for a crime in Chicago." Jackie says.

"We want no part of Frank." adds Susanne.

Travis inquires, "If I am representing you, I'd advise you to speak with the police. Who is Frank?"

The phone rings in his office, which is 90 by 120 feet with files everywhere, a safe, and a computer. His staff includes a secretary, who is five foot with pretty blue eyes, long blond hair, and a slim figure, and Willy Rose, the head lawyer, who is five foot ten inches tall and 245 pounds with short blond hair and brown eyes.

The secretary, Mrs. Johnson, picks up the receiver, saying, "Hello, can we help you?"

"We need to see Travis, please."

"He's busy now. Can you call back?" Mrs. Johnson replies.

When she hung up, Travis asks his three new clients, "What's going on?"

Jackie says, "Frank Zuccini is my husband, but there was a crime in Chicago."

"What happened?"

"What happened was that we used to be in vending, so we were in Chicago for the conference. While there, we told management that we had valuables in the vault, but that's a lie." says Susanne.

"Let me get this straight; you walk into the vault area and say you've come for your valuables. Is that right?" asks Travis.

Peggy says, "That's how it happened."

"Ladies, let's take this one step at a time." Travis instructs in a grave tone. "You need to turn yourselves in to the police, and they'll investigate your story. Where is the hotel?"

"We stayed at the Holiday Inn, and Frank is blind." Jackie explains.

💰

I'm with Rick, Tim, and George at Scott's Party, which has drugs, women, and booze along with loud rock music.

"How are you doing? Are you all right?" Tim asks me, noticing my anxious demeanor and shifty eyes.

"I'm feeling good." I tell him, but that's a lie. I'm still depressed, paranoid, and mad inside because Jackie, Susanne, and Peggy left me on my own.

"You need a drink?" asks Scott.

"That would be sweet." I say. I was drunk, high, and ready to commit the next crime.

"Let's go to the car." George suggests.

Scott comes over as we were leaving and says, "Thanks for coming by. Hope to see you again, Frank." We shake hands.

The four of us climb into Tim's car, which is a Ford Focus filled with clothes and his CD collection, and the radio is blaring. George sits in the passenger seat, while Rick and I sit in back. The weather is chilly—around 35 degrees—with a little drizzle.

"I need food and a smoke. Let's stop at the party store, Tim."

"I don't have any money, but we'll get it for you." Tim answers while nodding at Geroge and Rick. They know what to do.

George says, "If you agree, Rick and I will go in the store while you and Tim stay in the car because the getaway will be faster."

$\textbf{\$}$

John and Steve are still investigating while a month or two has gone by.

"How are things going?" asks Captain Edwards.

Steve says, "We interviewed all persons involved with the vendor convention. Some were in their rooms and others were in the lobby bar."

The phone rings, and Captain Edwards picks up the receiver. "Hello, this is Captain Edwards. Can we help you?"

"This is Mr. Nick Drake, director of the vending program."

"What's on your mind?" asks Captain Edwards.

"I may have information regarding the hotel robbery."

Captain Edwards replies, "We need to see you."

"I can come in tomorrow." Mr. Drake confirms.

The next day, Mr. Drake meets with Captain Edwards, John, and Steve.

"We kicked Frank Zuccini out of the vending program because he stole money and other items from machines and marked invoices paid when the suppliers were not paid." Mr. Drake explains.

"Can you give a description of Mr. Zuccini's height and weight?" asks Steve.

"Frank is five feet and four inches tall and maybe 185 pounds. He has brown hair and blue eyes." Mr. Drake continues, "It's a shame because we didn't think he would go that far and we think the reason is that Frank is behind on his bills and mortgage."

John and Steve look over their notes, and John says, "We thank you for your time; we know you're busy. Call us here if you need anything."

Mr. Drake gets up from his chair, shakes hands with the three policemen, and walks out of the office.

$

Rick starts to talk when the radio stops playing blues music, cutting him off, and leaving us all silent.

"We interrupt your regularly scheduled program to bring you this update. The police and federal agents are looking for Frank Zuccini, suspected in the Holiday Inn robbery in Chicago. Frank is considered dangerous, and if you have any information about where he is please call the authorities."

"It sounds like we better go to the store quickly." says Rick.

Tim, Rick, and George are packing guns when we get to our destination on Coal Hollow Road.

"We'll be back." says George as he and Rick exit the car.

The two men enter the store, which is full of racks and a couple coolers.

"Give us all your money and hurry." Rick demands to the lady standing near the register. She is shocked and shaking, but hands the two men all the money while I sit in the car talking with Tim about sports.

"How about those Cubs?" I comment excitedly.

"They're not better than the Cardinals, but we like the Bears." Tim says.

Just then, we hear sirens as Rick and George dash to the car with money, food, and cigarettes.

"Step on it." George commands as the two dive into the Ford's open doors.

"We're gone with the wind." Rick laughs.

As the car speeds away, shots are fired that narrowly miss the vehicle while the car is moving at 100 miles per hour.

"That was close." I say with relief.

"I told you we'd get lucky this time." explains Rick.

$

In Nebraska, Jackie, Susanne, and Peggy are in police custody. Fingerprints are taken, and all three ladies are jailed, awaiting trial back in Illinois. The cells are six by eight feet cages with steel frame beds and foam mattresses. "This is a rough life." says one woman across the jail.

$

Captain Edwards speaks, "You guys have any prints or DNA results?"

"Yes sir." says Steve. "We show Frank Zuccini as one of the vendors."

The phone rings, "Hello, this is Officer John Schnyder."

"This is the Nebraska authorities." replies the captain on the other line.

John turns toward Captain Edwards. "This is Captain Daniels from Nebraska. He wants to talk to you."

"This is Captain Edwards. Can we help you?"

Captain Daniels replies, "Yes, we have three ladies in custody. They were part of the hotel robbery in Chicago."

"I'll have two investigators come there to conduct interviews."

"That will be a pleasure, sir." Captain Daniels says.

Captain Edwards hangs up the phone, and Steve asks, "What's up, sir?"

The phone rings again, and Captain Edwards says, "Hang on a minute." He picks up the receiver. "Hello this is Captain Edwards."

"This is the East Peoria police. We spotted Frank Zuccini and his friends leaving a convenient store."

"My investigators will be there." Captain Edwards tells them.

John and Steve are told to leave for East Peoria, and then to Nebraska to conduct their part of the investigation.

$

I start to panic during all the action.

"Hold on, Frank. It'll be all right." George comforts.

"Don't worry; we got your back." adds Rick.

Tim mentions that he's hungry and wants pizza.

"Pizza Hut sounds good, and I'm hungry too." I say.

We pull up to Pizza Hut and order one pepperoni and two supreme pizzas and drive away without paying for them.

$

Paul and Dorris are together at Paul's house in Nebraska, eating dinner and visiting.

"What happened with Frank?" asks Paul.

"Frank is behind on his bills; now he's on the run, and I don't know where Jackie, Susanne, and Peggy are. Have you heard anything?"

"The radio reported that Jackie, Susanne, and Peggy are waiting to be sent back to Illinois to be charged with the hotel robbery, and that authorities are still looking for Frank."

The phone rings in the other room.

"I'll get it." says Dorris, as she dashes for the phone. "Hello. Hello."

"This is Frank, letting you know I am okay."

Dorris asks, "Where are you? What's going on?"

"Never mind that now." I say. "I know I'm being watched and heard on the phone." I click off.

"Who was that Dorris, and what's going on?" Paul asks, worried.

"That was Frank. He said he was being watched and maybe heard on the phone and didn't say where he is."

"We'll pray about this and get Frank some help."

💰

"How did you know where your brother and sister are?" Tim asks me.

"Paul lives in Nebraska, and Dorris was there visiting. I'm sure they heard the same news."

"Let's head to Georgia near the Florida border." says George.

"No one is to know where we are." Tim states.

We all shake hands in agreement.

💰

The first stop is East Peoria, Illinois, where officers Steve and John meet with Lieutenant Sorrenson, a man just short of six feet tall, weighing 200 pounds, and wearing a gray suit with the a pinstriped jacket.

"Glad to meet you guys." says Lieutenant Sorrenson.

The three men shake hands.

"We're here because you think Frank Zuccini was mixed up in a store robbery, is that right?" asks Steve.

"Yes, sir, witnesses saw a blind man in the car when they got away."

"We have copied a report that Frank is behind on his bills, and robbed the Holiday Inn in Chicago." says John.

The three policemen take notes, exchange cards, get up from their chairs, and leave the office.

"If you have any information, give us a call and let our captain know." Steve says.

John and Steve go to the airport, a large area with an electronic sidewalk and escalators. They're to go to Nebraska and meet with Captain Daniels, a man of six foot, gray hair, blue eyes, and 175 pounds. He is wearing a sports coat and multi-colored slacks. He is waiting at the airport when John and Steve fly in on a sixty-passenger plane.

"Hi, I'm Steve Davis, and this is my partner John Schnyder." The men shake hands.

"Glad you can come." says Captain Daniels.

"We're glad to meet you and we were told there were three ladies to be interviewed as part of our investigation." says Steve.

"Yes, sir. Jackie Zuccini and her two daughters turned to us with their story. They're in jail waiting to be sent back to Illinois."

"Show us the way," says John.

They hop into Captain Daniels's SUV that has a mobile TV. The three men ride to the office, which smells like it'd been remodeled. It's thirty by thirty feet with a conference room. They enter and sit down.

Captain Daniels says to the desk sergeant, "Bring in the three ladies, please."

The phone rings, and Captain Daniels picks up the receiver. "Hello, this is Captain Daniels. Can we help you?"

"This is attorney Travis Fitzpatrick, and I want to be there when you interview the three women."

"I'm sorry, sir. We've got two officers from Chicago here now to conduct their side of the investigation."

"I'll be there."

"Thank you, sergeant. We're waiting for their lawyer," says Captain Daniels.

Jackie, Susanne, and Peggy talk for a while.

"What becomes of us?" asks Peggy.

"You see, Peg, we have to face whatever sentence there is and move on with our lives, and maybe Frank will straighten out his life." answers Jackie.

"Whatever." says Susanne.

"Excuse me, ladies. Ready for your interview?" asks Captain Daniels.

The three women and Travis enter the office.

"Sit down. Let's get to the point." says Captain Daniels. "These two policemen are here from Chicago to take down your story that you told me."

"Hi. I'm John Schnyder, and this is Steve Davis. Tell us what happened."

The ladies are nervous, and Jackie says, "We were at the vending convention and decided to rob the hotel. Frank thought we could get away with it, but we feel guilty."

Susanne adds, "We walked in single file to the vault area and told the managers we had valuables kept there."

"Frank's cane acts as a weapon; they thought we had guns." Peggy says.

Steve and John take notes on their clipboard. Steve asks, "Can you think of any more details?"

The interview continues while the weather outside is getting cold and misty with a slight chance of flurries. There is tension in the room during the interview.

Jackie says, "Frank took off with his friends, Tim Masters, George Powel, and Rick Atkins. I don't know what happened to them when we left."

Steve asks, "Are you sure you're not lying to us?"

Travis says, "Look, these ladies had the courage to turn themselves in, and you accuse them of lying. Check your facts, gentlemen."

Offended, Steve says, "You're overstepping your boundaries. You do your job in court, and we'll handle the investigation."

"What happened before you got here?" Captain Denials asks, changing the subject.

John answers, "We made a trip to Peoria, Illinois, and interviewed witnesses to a convenient store robbery. We think these ladies know something about the details."

"That's right." Steve adds. "We've seen the store, and prints were left from two men. Unfortunately, there was no surveillance tape."

John says, "Witnesses said a blind man was in the car that is described as a Ford Focus."

Captain Daniels says, "Gentlemen, you're pretty thorough. When was the robbery?"

"The robbery was November 20th, and the women left on November 23rd." Steve answers.

"That's right, Steve, because the local sheriff served their eviction notice on November 23rd, and they were still in the house."

Steve continues, "We found overdue bills and the hotel contents in their home."

"The stash was from the hotel robbery." Jackie confesses. "Frank and I had an argument, and he took off when his buddies were contacted."

John says, "We have more information that there's been a robbery at the convenient store on Coal Hollow Road in East Peoria, Illinois, and shots were fired in the rain."

Steve asks, "What do these other guys look like?"

"One guy was African American, really tall and thin, and bald." Susanne answers. "The other guy was a few inches shorter and heavyset with cornrows and tattoos covering his arms."

Peggy says "The third guy was of average build with red hair and brown eyes."

Tim, Rick, George and I are watching baseball on TV when the news interrupts the game.

"We interrupt your regularly scheduled program for this special report. Authorities are securing a nationwide manhunt for Frank Zuccini and three other men. They're extremely dangerous to others and were last seen leaving the area of a store robbery in Illinois. If you have any information, contact your local authorities, and anyone hiding these men may be prosecuted."

I blurt out, "Let's go, guys! Forget the sports. We're getting out of here."

We hurry out of the old hotel, which smells of stale cigarettes, musty booze, and mildew. A crowd has gathered, and they're shouting, "That's him! That's him!" as we hurry away in a stolen SUV.

"Is there somebody following us? Look back." I bark.

Tim says, "It's okay, Frank. I can see behind me; there's no one there."

I still think someone is there, but Rick and George reassure me, saying, "We've never lied to you, Frank. Why should we start now?"

"We're going to Mexico, and no one is to find out." Tim plans.

The SUV smells brand new, and it has an iPod and speakers in the front, on the doors, and in back.

The news is heard while the three women are being grilled for more information.

"Are you sure there's been no contact with Frank since the Illinois robbery?" Steve accusingly questions.

Jackie says, "We admit we left after the robbery, but he hasn't been home, and he never called to say anything."

John says, "Well, ladies, we thank you for your time, and if your story checks out, there'll be no perjury charges. Here are our cards, and we'll be on our way."

The four men and three ladies get up from their chairs and exchange handshakes. Steve and John leave the station, get in their taxi, and go back to Chicago with their reports. The weather outside is cloudy, but cooperative for their flight.

$

Captain Edwards is at his desk when the phone rings and he picks up the receiver. "Hello, this is Captain Edwards. Can we help you?"

John says, "We're back and on the way to the office with more information."

Captain Edwards hangs up the phone and sifts through his emails while he waits for John and Steve to enter the office. "I'm glad you made it. Let's see what's going on."

Steve and John make copies and read their reports.

Captain Edwards says, "I notice the interview did well in Nebraska, which, by the way, the court ordered a bus to transport the ladies back to Chicago."

"Yes, sir, they were very cooperative, and their story checked out." Steve replies.

"I've got tons of emails saying that we're not doing our best. How can a visually impaired man—" The phone rings, interrupting him. "Damn it!" Edwards yells as he pounds his fist on the desk and picks up the receiver, putting the phone on speaker. "Hello, this is Captain Edwards!"

The voice says, "If you're looking for Frank, I would advise you to stay away, or he'll kill himself. Don't worry about who I am because it doesn't matter." The phone clicks.

Steve and John overhear the warning and say, "We didn't have time for the call to be traced."

Paul and Dorris are in Paul's living room when they call the Chicago police on a cold and rainy night. John, Steve, and Captain Edwards are in the office when the phone rings.

"We would like to talk to someone about Frank and does anyone know where he is? Where are Jackie, Susanne and Peggy?" Paul inquires.

Captain Edwards looks at his caller ID and says, "So your name is Paul Zuccini. Is there anyone there with you?"

Dorris says, "I'm on the phone. We're Frank's brother and sister, and we want to find Frank."

"We need to talk in person. Can you come and meet with us?"

"We would be glad to." Dorris answers. "Paul and I are worried about his wife and two daughters. Where are they, and what happened?"

"Jackie, Susanne, and Peggy are being transferred to Chicago for charges of robbing a hotel."

💰

My friends and I are riding through Oklahoma and Texas toward the border in order to cross into Mexico. I have an advantage because my Spanish-speaking skills are good enough.

"Tim, did you get the cops?" I ask.

"You would kill yourself if they came near." Tim repeats.

George points. "Look at that Mexican girl. Let's pick her up, and she'll help us cross the border."

We pull over to meet her, and I say, "Hola, miss, need a ride?"

The girl is dainty with dark hair and brown eyes. She is wearing a red blouse, white pants, and says, in Spanish, "No, thank you."

"Come here!" I demand.

Rick and George grab the girl along with her purse, and force her into the SUV. She is shaking and whimpering as we try to communicate with her.

"You're to help us cross the border, Maria." George forcefully instructs. The name Maria was written on her purse. She shakes her head. "Not understand," she says.

I respond, "We need to get into Mexico now!"

George gets in front to drive while Tim gets in back with me and the girl. She tenses up and screams, "No! No!"

Tim grabs her, pulls down her pants, and forces himself on her while she continues shrieking.

When Tim is done, he says, "She understood that."

We drive to a Mexican hotel with an old smell, worn out carpeting and dusty rooms. I say in Spanish to the manager, "We need a room for four people."

$

Paul and Dorris are ushered into the Captain Edwards's where John and Steve are also seated. "Glad to meet you folks." says Captain Edwards. "We're waiting for Jackie, Susanne, and Peggy to arrive. You can see them at the prison."

Dorris says, "What happened? I didn't think they would go that low."

"We're Steve Davis, John Schnyder, and Captain Edwards. The reason they're here is because the Holiday Inn was robbed, and they are waiting for trial."

Peggy, Susanne, and Jackie are getting off the bus with Travis who says, "Remember ladies, the plea is not guilty because there was no intent to rob the hotel. I'll claim that Frank masterminded the whole thing, and we think he was involved in the convenient store robbery."

"We realize the consequences of the crime." Jackie answers.

Travis's phone rings as they make their way to the prison, and he picks it up. "This is Travis."

"We're interviewing Frank's relatives. Do the ladies feel up to seeing them?" Captain Edwards asks.

"I'll ask them." Travis responds, putting his hand over the receiver. "Do you ladies want to see Frank's relatives?"

Susanne answers, "Not right now. We'll see them later while we go through court."

Jackie, Susanne, and Peggy talk amongst themselves. Peggy asks, "What's next for us, Mother?"

Jackie says, "We've got Benny and Christine praying for us, but the jury has to decide what's next."

"Paul and Dorris are worried, but I hope they understand we don't need to see them now." Susanne comments.

The warden makes an appearance. He's a large man—almost seven feet tall, with red hair and hazel eyes. In a deep voice, matching his appearance, he says, "You have a phone call. Which one of you ladies will take it?"

"I will take it." Jackie volunteers.

Warden Patterson leads Jackie to the phone.

"Hello, who is this?" asks Jackie.

"It's Benny. We will be there when the trial starts; don't forget."

Jackie says, "Okay, my son. Pray for me, Susanne, and Peggy."

💰

"You guys still around? What do we do with the girl?"

"It's okay, Frank." Rick says. "We're all here, and we'll take care of the girl. Let's go guys."

The four of us ditch the SUV and steal a 1998 minivan.

"Okay, guys. We drop the girl off in the woods," says Tim.

Tim, Rick, and George drag the girl out of the van, with all the cash stolen from her purse, and George commands her to, "Get to moving."

The weather is sunny and extremely humid. We get back in the van and hurry back to the run-down hotel. Some Spanish music on the radio is interrupted by the local news. "Mexican authorities are looking for Frank Zuccini and his friends. They are armed and dangerous, and if you have any information, please contact the authorities."

"Let's go guys, we're going to find another hotel." I say.

We hurry out to the next hotel. The hotel reeks of rotted wood, cheap booze, stale cigarettes, and body odor. There's frayed carpeting on the floor.

"Oh man," I exhale. "I hope no one followed us." The other three men look around.

"No one followed us. It'll be all right." Time reassures me.

Suddenly, a gunshot rings through the window.

Rick shouts, "Get down, Frank!"

Everyone gets down on the ground except George. Another shot comes through the window, hitting George. He slumps backward like he was sawed in half. "My chest! My chest!" he yells and dies there on the floor.

Tim and Rick look up as I yell, "George! George!"

Tim shakes his head, "It's no use."

Tim and Rick look through the broken window.

"Stay down, Frank." Rick instructs. "We'll get these bandits."

The two bandits burst into the room with guns in hand. One of them says in Spanish, "We want your money!"

Rick and Tim grab at the bandits, take the guns out of their hands, and begin beating them with their fists.

"This is for our friend!" Rick yelps. The bandits are struggling with my friends as the fists continue flying, but it ends when Rick grabs a gun. Shots are fired as both robbers fall to the floor face down.

"You stupid bandits." Tim spits. There is blood sprayed all over the room. Tim grabs me by the arm to help me up, and we hurry out of the hotel into the woods.

Rick says, "We are lucky the cops weren't there."

"That's for sure, Rick." I answer.

Captain Edwards and his unit look at emails from Mexican law enforcement, and he decides to call the Mexican authorities.

"Hello," answers Captain Rodriguez in broken English.

"You left messages for us to call you."

"Yes, Captain Edwards, there was a shooting at a hotel. We have three men dead, a tall, skinny, bald guy and two short Hispanic men."

"The tall man may be George Powel. Is he African American?"

"Yes, sir."

"Who are the other two?"

"The other two men are Mexican, but we're doing what we can to find Frank and his other friends."

"Thanks for the information, Captain Rodriguez."

Peggy, Susanne, and Jackie are scheduled for a court appearance in January. Their lawyer, Travis, says, "Ladies, you will be facing some questions from the prosecution, but answer them and try to keep your cool."

"We're ready for the consequences." Jackie solemnly claimed.

The lead prosecutor, Hank Jones, is wearing a striped suit with a white shirt. He says, "We plan to keep you ladies behind bars for a long time."

The courtroom is shaped like a movie theater with a slightly raised floor for the judge's bench and table. Judge Hart is seated at the table with a stern look in blue eyes and on his clean-shaven face that is surrounded with gray hair. The sleeve of his gray suit peaks out as he bangs his gavel on the table. "Order in the court!" he grumbles in a deep voice.

"The next case is the state versus Jackie, Susanne, and Peggy Zuccini. How do you plead?" asks Judge Hart.

Travis confidentally states, "Not guilty."

"Your trial will be in March."

$

It's March 20th, five months after the robbery. There's a crowd in the courtroom, including Benny and Christine, who cries, "Oh, Jack!"

"We're praying." Benny adds.

Judge Hart commands, "Order in the court!" and a hush falls over the crowd. "Ladies and gentlemen of the jury, you are about to weigh the evidence for or against these three defendants. Let me begin by saying that these defendants were alleged to rob a Holiday Inn of their valuables. There is to be no talking to the media, or anyone else about the case. Let's begin with opening statements."

Jones gets up and says, "Ladies and gentlemen of the jury, we have evidence showing that these ladies meant to rob the hotel the night of October 12th. We hope that you're fair in convicting these ladies."

Fitzpatrick stands up to speak, "Ladies and gentlemen of the jury, understand that the prosecution may try to twist the story in their favor to convict these ladies. We hope that you're fair in letting these ladies get their life back."

Paul and Dorris are also in the crowd during the proceedings.

"The prosecution will call their first witness." Judge Hart declares.

Jones says, "Actually, Your Honor, before I call Captain Daniels to the stand, I need to state that Travis Fitzpatrick has a conflict of interest in this case. We have evidence to show that Mr. Fitzpatrick may have represented other witnesses in prior cases that are set to testify against Jackie, Susanne, and Peggy. Would you appoint a new defense attorney?"

"Sidebar gentlemen." Judge Hart says.

The two lawyers argue with each other as they approach the podium, and Judge Hart interrupts them, saying, "Mr. Fitzpatrick, you are excused from the case due to your record of previous cases. We're appointing Donald Shafer."

The two lawyers walk away, and trial is back in session. Donald Shafer, a tall, slender man with dark hair and brown eyes, takes his spot, relieving Fitzpatrick.

Jones says, "The prosecution calls Captain Daniels to the stand."

Captain Daniels makes his way to the podium.

"Raise your right hand, please," Judge Hart requests. "Do you swear to tell the truth, and nothing but the truth?"

"Yes, Your Honor."

"State your name and why you're here."

"My name is Captain Luke Daniels, and I'm here from Nebraska because Jackie, Susanne, and Peggy Zuccini turned themselves in to me. They told me about the robbery. Frank Zuccini is the mastermind behind everything happening here."

Jones asks, "What are the details of the robbery?"

"I was told that there were valuables in the vault at the Holiday Inn, so they decided to rob the hotel."

"Mr. Shafer," Judge Hart begins. "Do you need to cross-examine this witness?"

"Yes, Your Honor. Captain Daniels, is it true that these women are sorry because of the crime they've committed?"

"Yes, they told me they were sorry because they had fallen behind with their debts and were looking for a way to catch up."

"Objection!" Mr. Jones interjects. "The defense is trying to make it look like it's okay to rob the hotel!"

"Overruled. Any more questions?"

"No, Your Honor."

"You may step down, Captain Daniels. Do you have more witnesses?"

Jones speaks up. "We call Dave Anderson from the Holiday Inn."

The manager, Dave, walks up to the podium and sits down.

"State your name for the record."

"I am Dave Anderson, manager at the Holiday Inn."

"What are the details of the robbery?" Jones questions.

"There were four people that entered the vault area. They demanded to be taken to the valuables that they claimed were being held for them. The man had a cane, and we thought they had guns."

Jones asks, "Can you point out the defendants in the room?"

"Yeah I think they're right there." Dave points his finger toward the three ladies.

"Anything else you can tell us?"

"They were at the vendor convention for the blind." Dave adds.

"That is all," Jones says, sitting down.

"Does the defense have anything for this witness?"

Shafer answers, "Mr. Anderson, you aren't sure if there were two or three ladies when you interviewed with the police. Tell the truth, was it two women and two men, or was it three women and one man?"

Jones shouts, "Objection Your Honor. The defense is badgering the witness!"

"Overruled. Answer the question."

Dave says, "That's right. I wasn't sure because I was worried about my safety."

"You may step down, Mr. Anderson," Judge Hart says.

💰

I'm still on the run when the court breaks for lunch.

We hear the local Spanish music interrupted by an update. "We have information that Frank Zuccini's wife and two daughters are on trial for their role in a hotel robbery, but Frank is still missing. He's dangerous and has two friends with him. A million dollar reward is in place. If you have any information, please call the authorities."

"Crap. We need to start using Spanish names. Mine is Mario Escobar." I tell the guys.

Rick says, "Hey Mario, what are our names?"

"Tim, you are Jose Valdez, and Rick, you are Pedro Montez. Let the cops know that I'll kill myself if they come near."

"We'll tell them that you killed yourself." Rick schemes.

The humidity is high, and the temperature is nearly 90 degrees with the sun beaming through the window of the high-rise.

Captain Rodriguez is seated at his desk when the phone rings and he picks up the receiver. "Hello, this is Captain Rodriguez."

"Never mind who I am because Frank is dead."

"How did it happen?"

"He shot himself."

As Captain Rodriguez opens his mouth to respond, the caller hangs up and the line goes dead.

I'm sitting on the couch in an old high-rise that is frequently used by Mexican gangs. The smells of death, weed, musky odor, and booze fill the building. Tim and Rick are watching the bullfight.

"Look at those guys," laughs Rick.

"Yeah, that's sweet. All they're doing is running around the bull and stabbing it with spears," Tim says.

A few knocks come from the door and Rick forcefully whispers, "Get down, Frank!"

Tim and Rick draw their guns and stare at the door. "Who is it?" asks Rick.

"Let me in we need to talk," the stranger responds.

Rick questions, "Frank, do you recognize his voice?"

I think for a moment, "I think it's Tom Milner. He's a family friend."

"Hold on. We're coming," says Tim.

They open the door to reveal Tom standing there, a man of five foot three, 185 pounds, with blond hair and blue eyes.

"I'm glad to see you, Tom, but what are you doing here?"

"I came here on vacation, but I've been hearing your name all over the news so I came to find you. I figured you would be hiding out in a high-rise like in the old stories we used to listen to on the radio. There's a million dollar reward out for you."

"Grab him, guys," I instruct Rick and Tim.

"Hold everything, sir. Empty all your pockets, or we shoot," commands Tim.

Tom hesitates, then says, "We need to stay together." A shot comes from Tim's gun, and Tom falls to the floor.

"Empty his pockets. He may have been sent by the cops," I say.

Rick and Tim go through his clothes. They find several wads of one hundred dollar bills, a gun, and a listening device.

"We dump the body out the window, Tim," I instruct as we carry the corps through the window and let go.

The trial is back in session, and Judge Hart resumes his position. "Order in the court! Call your next witness."

Jones says, "I call on John Schnyder from the Chicago Police Department."

John comes to the podium.

"Raise your right hand. You swear to tell the truth so help you God?" asks Judge Hart.

John answers, "Yes, Your Honor."

Jones begins his questioning. "What happened when you heard about the robbery?"

"Steve and I interviewed both managers, Mike and Dave. They told us that these women were in the vault area, along with a visually impaired man behind them. The women told the managers that they had valuables that were kept. Some of the other crowd saw them leaving the scene in a hurry."

"Were you told about their height and weight by the managers?"

"No sir."

"Ladies and gentlemen, the document we're showing is that of Officers John Schnyder and Steve Davis,"

"Does Mr. Shafer have any questions?" Judge hart asks.

Shafer begins his questioning. "We understand that you interviewed these ladies. Isn't it true that you think they're lying?"

"Objection. That is hearsay," says Jones.

"If you're not telling the truth, you could be charged with perjury," warns Shafer.

"Objection, Your Honor!" Jones exclaims.

"Sustained. Please rephrase the question, Mr. Shafer," Judge Hart says.

"Mr. Schnyder, what makes you think that these ladies are involved in other crimes?" asks Shafer.

"First of all, they know about the convenient store after Jackie's husband left. They were evicted from their home because of overdue payments. We found all the stash in the house."

"Without a court order?" Schafer accuses. "Your honor, I submit the evidence on the grounds that they were obtained without a court order."

A rumbling is heard throughout the crowd.

"Order in the court!" demands Judge Hart as the gavel bangs a few times. "The court is in recess until tomorrow. I'll make a decision about the evidence."

$

After the encounter with Tom, I'm feeling anxious and overwhelmed. "Get me outta here. There may be cops coming."

Rick, Tim, and I hurry to the street where we see another minivan. This one is a 1993, and we quickly steal it and get out of Mexico as fast as we can. We speed through Texas, and keep heading west toward Los Angeles, California.

"All this running is making me tired," Rick complains.

"Me too. Whatever, we have to keep going," says Tim.

The music is interrupted as the news comes through the van's stereo again. "This is a special report. Authorities are still looking for Frank Zuccini. His wife and two daughters are on trial today for a hotel robbery. Frank is blind, but considered dangerous to himself and others. He is described as being five feet and four inches tall, 185 pounds with brown hair and blue eyes. He is said to be with two friends. One is five foot ten and 190 pounds with red hair and brown eyes. The other is African American, five foot ten, and 235 pounds. If you have any information, please contact the authorities."

I sigh. My anxiety is accelerating.

"Hey, look! There's Universal Studios!" Rick shouts, pointing out the window.

I hear a car revving behind us and am extremely paranoid. "I think someone is following us." I say.

"Frank, we'll be all right," reassures Rick just before I hear a loud bang that shakes the van.

"Oh man, we have a flat," says Tim.

Tim spots a tire shop nearby and says, "I'm going in," as he dashed out of the van and went in.

"This is a holdup, so hand over a tire with a sixteen-inch rim and all the money. I mean business!" Tim yells the manager.

The man behind the counter pulls out a gun, but Tim raises his gun and shoots the man before he can do anything. He falls to the ground like he was on hinges.

"Oh man, I heard a shot!" I say.

"Here comes Tim," Rick says as Tim dashes to the car and hops in.

"That was close! The guy tried to shoot, but my gun went off first."

"We made it," says Rick as we ride on the flat while sirens are getting closer. We escape to an area loaded with redwoods large enough for a vehicle to drive through. Rick and Tim change the tire, and we disappear into a cheap motel.

💰

The crowd gathers as court resumes to continue the trial on a sunny and pleasant day. Judge Hart bangs his gavel. "Order! Order in the court! Now that we're here, there is a court order along with other documents. You may continue, Mr. Shafer."

"Do you have anything else to suggest that these women were involved in other crimes?" Shafer asks Mr. Schnyder.

"We can only link them to the hotel."

"That is all," says Shafer.

"You may step down, Mr. Schnyder," says Judge Hart. "Will the prosecution call their next witness?"

Jones says, "The prosecution calls Captain Edwards to the stand."

Captain Edwards makes his way to the podium.

"Raise your right hand. Do you swear to tell the truth so help you God?" asks Judge Hart.

"Yes, Your Honor. I'm Captain Neal Edwards, head of the robbery detail in the Chicago police department."

Jones begins his questioning. "Can you tell us any details about what happened at the hotel?"

"Both managers told us the three defendants and a blind man entered the vault and said they had valuables kept there. We searched the home and found the contents of the robbery, along with overdue bills, and had them fingerprinted. As far as I'm concerned, they belong behind bars."

"Objection, Your Honor. The last statement should be struck from the record," Shafer declares.

"Sustained. Anything else you can tell us, Captain Edwards?"

"No, Your Honor."

Jones concludes, saying, "Thank you for your time. Your department is doing a great service."

"Do you have any questions for this witness?" Judge Hart asks Shafer.

"Captain Edwards, what makes you so sure that these defendants meant to rob the hotel?"

"Frank is missing, and we think they know where he is."

"That's a lie! You cops are getting paid to put me and my daughters behind bars!" Jackie screams with emotion.

Judge Hart bangs his gavel, "Order! Order in the court! One more outburst and you will be held in contempt."

"One more question, Your Honor." Shafer says. "Captain Edwards, is there a previous criminal record we're not aware of?"

"We did a background check and found no previous record."

"You may step down, Captain Edwards. This court is adjourned until tomorrow," says Judge Hart.

The courtroom empties and the defendants are led back to their cells.

Tim says, "Mario, let's go to the Lakers game."

"Wait, my name is what?" Rick asks.

"Your name will be Pedro." I answer.

Rick says, "We'll have a good time at the game."

We find the LA arena and go to the game without a problem.

"Look at that jump shot," Tim comments.

"That's cool how Ray Allen is defending Lamar Odem," replies Rick.

"Who's there?" I scream.

"Hey! It's okay," replies Rick.

"I'm sorry," I tell him, "but I'm still worried.

$

Captain Edwards, John, and Steve are in Captain Edwards's office when the phone rings.

"Hello, this is Captain Edwards."

"This is the LA police," says Captain Lucas on the line. "We think that Frank was seen running around LA."

"John and Steve will fly out to meet you," reports Captain Edwards. He hangs up the phone and turns to the men, "You have your orders gentlemen. You're to go to Los Angeles and investigate where Frank and his two friends could be."

John and Steve board a plane bound for LA.

Captain Dan Lucas is a muscular, six foot African American man, weighing 220 pounds. He waits as John and Steve arrive by rental car.

"Hi, glad to meet you," says Captain Lucas with a strong voice. "Now then, my office is over here."

The three men enter the building and walk down the hall to Captain Lucas's office, which smells of coffee, doughnuts, and other food items. He has an assortment of awards hanging inside a display case.

"We'll help as best as we can," says Steve.

"Yes, sir. Frank is famous, but for the wrong reason," John adds.

"I'm in touch with the Mexican government, but they have not turned up anything, except they got a call from a man who said Frank killed himself," Captain Lucas informs them.

"Were you told if the gentleman was white or African American?" asks Steve.

"Yes they said a white man's voice was on the phone."

"That fits our suspect Tim Masters." says John. "Can you tell us why you think Frank may be in LA?"

"There was a robbery at a tire shop near Universal Studios. A man was shot and killed and a blind man was seen in the car talking to another man," reports Captain Lucas.

"Do you have any description reports?" Steve asks.

"Here in my file." Captain Lucas reaches in his file and hands the reports to John and Steve.

"Interesting. They include the reports from Mexico and match who we're looking for. Would you make us some copies?" asks Steve.

"Right away, gentlemen."

After copies are made, the policemen set out to interview witnesses around the tire shop.

$

The announcers interrupt the basketball game to ask, "Will Frank Zuccini come to the front desk?"

"Let's go," Tim says.

We get out into the parking lot and spot a brand new blue Mustang. Rick bashes in the window, and Tim begins to hotwire the car. Within minutes, the three of us hurry away in the stolen mustang.

"Be careful of those tracking devices," Rick warns.

"You got that right," I respond.

"Look out, Frank!" Tim shrieks.

Suddenly, I hear sirens as we speed away. "Get to moving," I bark to the others.

"Hold on, Frank!" Tim says as the car roars up to 100 mph.

$

The phone rings on Captain Lucas's waist. "Hello, what's going on?"

"Captain, it's Frank and his friends," reports the officer. "They got away again."

After hanging up, Captain Lucas says to John and Steve, "They chased Frank and his friends, but they got away."

"Where were they?" asks John.

"They were at the Lakers game, and witnesses recognized them."

$

Court resumes the following day, and Judge Hart bangs his gavel. "Do you have anything else for this witness, Mr. Shafer?"

"No, Your Honor; that is all."

"You can step down, Captain Edwards. Next witness please."

Jones pauses for a moment. "The prosecution calls Mr. Nick Drake."

Mr. Drake makes his way to the podium.

"Raise your right hand, do you swear to tell the truth?"

"Yes, Your Honor."

"State your name and occupation."

"I'm Nick Drake, director of the vending program for the blind."

Jones asks, "How well do you know these defendants?"

"I have seen them several times at the convention. I admit I'm surprised they're here today."

"Why are you surprised?"

"Because, for one thing, I didn't think these ladies were desperate enough to commit a crime like that. They seem so nice."

"You knew they lied to investigators saying they had nothing to do with the crime, is that right?" asks Jones.

"Objection, Your Honor. The prosecution is trying to put words in the witness's mouth," Shafer says.

"Statement withdrawn."

"Please continue, Mr. Jones," Judge Hart says.

"Were you aware that these defendants lied to investigators?" Jones asks again.

"I had no idea that they committed a crime until I heard the news."

"Thank you, Mr. Drake. That's all."

"You have any questions, Mr. Shafer?" asks Judge Hart.

Shafer asks, "Mr. Drake, you said you're surprised that these ladies committed a crime. Do you believe they're a threat to society?"

"No I don't. I thought from the beginning they seemed nice to other people and fell on hard times. They would like to straighten their lives out and move on."

"That's all, Mr. Drake," says Shafer.

"You can step down, Mr. Drake. Does the prosecution have any more witnesses?"

"No, Your Honor. The prosecution rests its case," replies Jones.

"The court resumes with the defense tomorrow. We are adjourned."

$

Relaxation comes after we escape from the cops, but I'm still worried inside.

Tim asks, "Would you order our food at McDonald's? You have a better memory."

"Sweet. What do you guys want?" I ask.

Tim requests a Big Mac and a large Pepsi, and Rick says he wants an Angus burger with everything, including lettuce and tomato, fries, and a large Pepsi. We drive up to the window, and I place the order. We grab our food in a hurry and drive off without paying or being recognized.

"That was cool, Frank. We got that for free," says Rick. "We'll disappear into the high-rise around the corner."

$

John, Steve, and Captain Lucas return to the office as the phone rings. "Hello, this is Captain Lucas."

"Yes, sir, this is Captain Rodriguez in Mexico. We have the girl that Frank and his two buddies picked up and took across the border."

"Captain Rodriguez, I have Officers John Schnyder and Steve Davis from Chicago here with me."

"Yes, sir, I spoke with Captain Edwards," says Captain Rodriguez. "He wants them to talk to Maria."

"Did she say what happened?" asks Captain Lucas.

"She said she was kidnapped, raped, and kicked out without her purse in Mexico. Maria will be there to see you in LA." says Captain Rodriguez.

"We'll be waiting," says Captain Lucas. He hangs up and addresses the officers, "Well, gentlemen, we're that much closer to catching the man and his two friends. The girl will be here to help us find him."

Maria Garcia arrives by plane paid for by the Mexican government. Captain Lucas and the two investigators are there to greet her at the airport.

"I'm happy to meet you," she says to the policemen.

"We'll escort you to the office. You can have some coffee," says Lucas.

Maria is handed a cup of coffee as John says, "Now let's get to the point. What were the details of the kidnapping?"

Maria cries a little and says, "I'm sorry, but it's not easy to talk about. The blind guy asked me if I needed a ride. Then his two buddies grabbed me and dragged me into the SUV. The other white guy raped me."

"Was there anything else during your ordeal?" Steve asks.

"Yeah, the African American guy said that they needed help crossing the border."

"Were there three or four men?" asks Captain Lucas.

"There was four guys."

"The report we have, Captain Lucas, is that one of the suspects was killed during a fight at a Mexican hotel," explains Steve.

"Thank you, Maria. You have been very helpful," Captain Lucas says. "If we get this man, you may have to testify in court. We have a room for you at the local hotel. You'll be safe there."

"Thank you very much," Maria says.

💰

I never thought I would be in this position. Tim, Rick, and I decided that LA was too much.

"Where do we run to now?" asks Rick.

"Let's plan on going to New York," Tim replies.

We all agree and take off to the airport bound for New York using our Spanish names.

💰

Captain Lucas is at his desk when his phone rings. "Hello, it's Captain Lucas. Can I help you?"

"Hi, it's Steve. John and I located Frank and his two companions, and they're on their way to New York."

"I'll contact the New York authorities right away, and they'll be picked up at the airport."

I notice something suspicious about the pilot speaking to the command center on the radio in the background. I nod at Tim to check it out. The three of us force our way into the cockpit.

"Excuse me, pilot, we want this plane diverted quickly," demands Tim.

The pilot looks surprised, "What do you mean diverted? This plane is bound for New York!"

"I said divert to Boston quickly, and no radio," Tim threatens.

"That's right, mister. We're serious, and no cops," adds Rick.

"We figured it out when we heard you on the radio. Quiet everyone, hand over your money, jewelry and cell phones." I say over the speaker. "When do we land in Boston?" I ask the pilot.

The pilot doesn't respond.

"Hey, my friend asked you a question." Rick says, pushing him.

"We'll be in Boston in about five hours," the pilot reluctantly answers.

A voice comes over the pilot's radio. "Control to plane fifty, is there a problem?"

"The pilot is busy now," says Rick. "You guys have a problem." Rick destroys the radio and a shot rings from the cockpit. The pilot falls in a heap off the side of his chair.

"Let that be a lesson. Anyone else want to be a hero?" Rick threatens.

Captain Edwards answers the ringing phone on his desk. "Hello, this is Captain Edwards."

"Hello Captain," says John. "We're in LA in a lot of traffic, but Frank and his two companions were spotted leaving on a plane for New York. Do you have any more information?"

"Yes, the FBI is involved, and I heard from New York," Captain Edwards answers. "The plane has not gotten there yet, and the radio isn't working. It's been hijacked."

"That's right sir," says Steve. "We were told by air traffic control that they're on the run and the plane is no longer headed for New York.

$

The next day, court resumes during the hijacking. Judge Hart bangs his gavel while demanding, "Order! Order in the court. There is a problem. One of the jurors has been excused because they talked to the media about the case. I have chosen an alternate juror. Please step up."

The proceedings continue after the delay. "Will the defense call their first witness," asks Judge Hart.

Shafer says, "We call Ben Zuccini to the stand."

The crowd groans a little, and the judge taps his gavel lightly on the table.

Benny says, "It's all right Christine. We'll get through this." He makes his way to the podium.

"Raise your right hand. Do you swear to tell the truth?" asks Judge Hart.

"I do, Your Honor," says Benny.

"State your name and occupation."

"I'm Ben Bracket, not Zuccini as mentioned. I manage a chemical plant in Nebraska."

Shafer asks, "Mr. Bracket, what led your mom and sisters to this point?"

"I think they were trying to make ends meet and they weren't making enough money in vending. There was discussion about moving to Nebraska to look for other jobs, but Frank wanted money right now to catch up on their mortgage and other bills."

"According to the prosecution, your family committed other crimes." says Shafer. "Have your mom and sisters been involved?"

"No, sir, my mom and sisters feel guilty about what they did. Frank is still missing and there is no contact."

"That is all," Shafer says.

"Any questions, Mr. Jones?" asks Judge Hart.

Jones stands, saying, "Ben, your mother and sisters intentionally committed robbery. Why are you here?"

"Objection, Your Honor," says Shafer. "The prosecution is trying to change the witness's mind."

"Sustained. Rephrase the question, Mr. Jones."

"What brings you here today? Are you getting paid?"

"Objection, Your Honor, the prosecution is accusing the witness of being paid to testify," Shafer argues.

"Sidebar, gentlemen." Judge Hart demands.

Both lawyers gather around the judge to speak.

"Mr. Jones, you are to rephrase the question. The last statement will be stricken from the record," says Judge Hart.

Court resumes and Jones asks, "Mr. Bracket, what brings you here today?"

"I'm surprised at my family for committing this crime because growing up I was taught that robbing was not the answer to making ends meet. That was wrong for Frank to bring them into this situation."

"No more questions, Your Honor," says Jones.

"You may step down, Ben."

There was a short break, as Benny makes it back to his seat.

"Are you all right?" asks Christine.

"Yes. Keep praying."

"Will the defense call their next witness?" asks Judge Hart.

Shafer looks at his list, and says, "The defense calls on Paul Zuccini."

A hush comes over the crowd as Paul makes his way to the podium.

"Raise your right hand. Do you swear to tell the truth so help you God?" Judge Hart asks.

"Yes, Your Honor."

"Your name and occupation?"

"I'm Paul Zuccini. My job is at a factory in Nebraska where I live."

Shafer asks, "Do you feel up to testifying for these defendants and against your brother?"

"Yes, sir, though I admit I'm surprised to be on the stand today. My sister and I heard the news and were surprised by the current events of the family. These defendants tried to make ends meet and got caught up doing the wrong thing to catch up on their bills."

"Was there a pattern to suggest that the crimes could have been prevented?"

"Yes, sir. My family was in vending and didn't make enough money to keep up with their mortgage and utilities. Maybe they could move to Nebraska where Frank could work at the factory."

"What kind of a factory hires blind people?"

"Toilet paper manufacturing."

"That is all," Shafer concludes.

"Any questions for this witness?" Judge Hart asks, looking at Jones.

"Mr. Zuccini, are you aware of any more crimes that these defendants are linked to?"

"No sir," answers Paul. "There was one call from Frank, but he didn't say where he was and these ladies had no contact with me. They wanted to wait and talk to me and Dorris when court was over."

"Are you aware of the fame your brother has caused by committing crime and the consequences of testifying against him?"

"Yes, sir. It's good for the family, and I pray every day that Frank may wake up and realize that crime doesn't pay."

Jones says, "That's all, Your Honor."

"You may step down, Mr. Zuccini. Ladies and gentlemen of the jury," Judge Hart continues. "It's now time for closing statements, and the jury will be secluded to weigh the evidence."

Jones says, "Ladies and gentlemen, the evidence you see before you proves without a doubt these defendants' intentions to commit the crime described. They were out to make a quick buck and take advantage of others."

Schafer challenges the previous statement with, "Ladies and gentlemen, the evidence before you shows how good people fall on hard times. The crime described was committed because these defendants are behind on their bills and Frank's blindness was used to make people felt empathize with the situation. There were no previous crime records for these individuals, and they were not intentionally taking advantage of anyone."

Judge Hart says, "Court is now adjourned, and the jury will take as much time as they need to weigh the evidence."

The courtroom empties and the defendants are led back to their cells.

💰

I sat with intense excitement waiting for the plane to land in Boston.

When the plane lands, Rick takes me by the arm to head one way while Tim goes in the other direction. Tim is recognized by the undercover cops in the crowd who quickly tackle him and get him in handcuffs. We never saw the cops pick him up. Rick and I hurry as fast as we can to the hotel where the three of us are supposed to meet, but Tim never shows. It doesn't take us long to figure out that Tim has been arrested.

"You know he'll testify against us, Frank," says Rick.

"That figures. Some friend he's turned out to be," I answer.

I am not familiar with Boston, but Rick says, "Look, Frank, our backs are against the wall. That's why we have to keep running. Let's get a cheesesteak."

Rick and I make our way to the Boston Market and each get a cheesesteak sandwich.

"We got to keep low, Frank. That means pay for our food."

"After we get our food, find the nearest high-rise." I say.

$

Tim is hauled away to Boston's federal prison to await bail. FBI Agent Robert Henderson, a man just over six feet tall and weighing 195 pound with light brown hair and blue eyes, questions, "You are Tim Masters, is that right?"

Tim looked stone-faced. "Why do you care? I'm not talking."

"We checked your background, Tim. We know that Frank was your high school buddy. You might get a lighter sentence if you talk now."

"That is too bad."

Agent Henderson gets on his phone, "This is Agent Henderson. I need to talk to Captain Edwards."

Captain Edwards picks up the phone. "Hi, Agent Henderson. You have information for me?"

"Yes, sir. I have Tim Masters in jail awaiting bail and trial. He's not talking, but we know he's been involved with Frank."

"When my officers get back, you may come meet with us," Captain Edwards suggests.

$

John and Steve arrive in Chicago to meet with Captain Edwards.

"How was your trip?" asks Captain Edwards.

Steve replies, "Very hectic. LA has a lot of traffic."

"We're to meet with FBI Agent Henderson, flying in from Boston. They have Tim Masters," Captain Edwards excitedly reports.

"Sweet! That's a break," says John. "Is he talking?"

"No, he refuses to talk."

"That means he takes all the rap for robbery and murder," Steve points out.

The phone rings again. "Hello, this is Captain Edwards."

"Yes, sir, this is Captain Rodriguez. Did you locate Frank?"

"No, but we've got his friend Tim." Captain Edwards responds. "We'll keep you posted."

FBI Agent Henderson arrives at the Chicago airport with Captain Edwards, Steve, and John there to greet him.

"Hi, I'm Robert Henderson, FBI Agent. Glad to meet you guys."

"It's a nice spring day full of fresh flowers and the sound of traffic" jokes Steve.

The four men get into the police SUV and go back to the office.

"Would you like a cup of coffee?" Captain Edwards offers Agent Henderson.

"Sure, that will be fine."

John says, "Agent Henderson, we have Frank's wife and two daughters on trial now for robbery. Does Tim have any clue about that?"

Agent Henderson grabs his cup of coffee and answers, "The suspect is stone-faced and shows no emotion. He refuses to talk because his life may be in danger."

Steve adds, "We've interviewed the Mexican girl who was kidnapped and raped by this suspect."

"Maybe she needs to see him face to face," suggests Agent Henderson.

💰

It's early April, the smell of fresh flowers and singing birds is about when the jury comes back with the verdict. The courtroom is filled with people awaiting the result and a lot of nervous tension.

"Order! Order in the court," says Judge Hart. "Foreman of the jury, what is the verdict?"

"Your honor, the jury found the defendants guilty, but remorseful."

A rush of sadness fills the courtroom.

"Will the defendants please rise? Sentencing will be in two weeks. We hope you've learned something along with a better understanding of the law. The court is now adjourned."

The three ladies are hysterically crying as the courtroom empties, and they are led back to their cells. "I'm very sorry," says Shafer. "We'll get you the lightest sentence we can get."

💰

The news comes through the radio again. "Authorities are on the lookout for Frank Zuccini and his friend Rick. They've been spotted in Boston. If you see these men, please don't hesitate to call. They're extremely dangerous, and we need them alive. If you have information, please contact the authorities right away."

Rick and I shiver and shrug our shoulders. "Well, Rick, I never thought of being in this position," I admit.

"We're in deep, Frank, but for now we're safe here." remarks Rick, looking around the twelfth floor of the old high-rise they've taken shelter in before he nods off to sleep.

$

It's a beautiful spring day outside filled with people in the streets, sounds of birds, and the fresh smell of flowers as Tim is sitting in his, cell staring at the bars. His face is hairy from not shaving for a few days.

"Hey dude!" an inmate yells at Tim. He is African American, stands about six feet tall, and weighs 200 pounds.

"Dude, you talking to me?" asks Tim.

"Yeah, I'm breaking outta here. You want to go?"

"Yeah dude. What's your name?"

"The name is Justin."

"I need to catch up to my friend Frank. He may be worried about me," says Tim.

"I know, man. I hear the news. We'll meet in the recreation yard and start a fight as a diversion. I got some guard uniforms for us to put on, and then we walk outside."

"That will be awesome."

"Cool," says Justin. "Look, I got a friend following where Frank is. He is supposed to visit me."

"Sweet. How do I know he's not a cop?"

"He's part of a gambling ring out in Vegas."

"Cool," says Tim.

$

I wake up in the high-rise filled with the smell of paint, cigarettes, marijuana, and booze to a knock at the door. Rick wakes up too. "Get down, Frank. I'll see who it is," he whispers.

"Who's there?" Rick barks.

The stranger says, "Open the door. We need to talk."

"Oh shit, I hope it's not the cops." Rick creeps toward the door with gun in hand. When he opens the door, the stranger blurts, "Calm down. I want to help you. I know where Tim is."

"Who are you, and what do you want?" I ask.

"Let me come in and talk."

"Hold your gun on him," I say to Rick.

"It's okay, man. You're covered." he reassures me. Then turning to the stranger he says, "Now mister, you're to be searched."

"Look, man, I got nothing to hide. There are no wires from the FBI or the cops. I'm part of a gambling ring in Vegas and heard the news. My friend Justin found your friend Tim to get him out to catch up to you guys."

"Whatever." says Rick doubtfully.

$

It's sunny and warm on April 20th, the day of sentencing for Jackie, Susanne and Peggy. The courtroom fills up with the crowd of friends and family.

"Order! Order in the court. Will the defendants please rise and remain standing. Since you have been found guilty by a jury of your peers, the sentence placed on you is one year in jail, and one year probation. You're to attend chaplain services and have a job while in jail. The probationary period is ten hours of community service a week, along with a part-time or full-time job."

Jackie, Susanne, and Peggy are crying as they are led away to their cells.

Peggy whines, "Thanks to stupid Frank we don't have a life."

"It's not good to blame him because we had something to do with the crime," Jackie says.

"That's right, mother." Susanne agrees.

Rick continues as I'm growing more and more concerned, "Well gambling man, where is Tim now?"

"He is in Boston federal prison, and my friend Justin is arranging for a breakout. I need to get back to him immediately."

"Let's go," I say.

Rick still has his gun pointed at the gambler as he leads the way out of the high-rise. We get to his car— a brand new Mercedes, loaded with mobile TV, stereo, and a laptop.

Rick says, "Nice ride. Hop in, Frank." We dash into the car, and head to the prison in time to see Tim and Justin running out of the gates as the alarm bell is going off.

"They're getting away!" shout the prison guards.

Tim and Justin jump into the car.

"That was close. I was worried you guys gave up on me," Tim says.

Rick replies, "I thought you would've gotten scared and spilled everything to the cops."

"I should know what a friend you are to me." I admit.

"It's all good."

I feel something cold and round poking the back of my head. "Hey, blind guy, you're part of us now," Justin says with a gun at my head.

"Hey! Hey, idiot, put down that gun!" Rick shouts.

"You don't treat my friend like that!" the gambler says to Justin. "I'll take care of this." He draws his gun and shoots Justin in the head. "I'm sorry. I didn't realize you're blind, Frank."

"There's no need to feel sorry for me. I get along just fine."

"I'll get you guys to Vegas, and from there you're on your own," the gambler says.

Tim and Rick look at each other and Rick asks, "What did the cops have to say, Tim?"

"One guy was an FBI agent who told me I would get a lighter sentence if I talk, but I said I wasn't talking."

"What do we do with the body?" I ask.

"I'll take care of him; he ratted on the mob," the gambler says.

He dumps the corps in a wooded area, returns to the car, and drives on.

"Did the cops say anything else?" I ask Tim.

"They kept hounding me about where you and Rick could be and telling me that there was a million dollar reward."

"Did you say a million dollars?" asks the gambler.

"None of your business," Tim replies. There is tension as the car screeches to a halt.

"Get out now!" yells the gambler.

"Hey, we're not in Vegas yet," I say.

"Get the hell out!" he repeats.

I hear a yell as Tim knocks the stranger in the head with my cane, and Rick's gunshot makes the gambler slump over.

"That's great; now we dump the body and the car. We get into a lot of bloody messes," says Rick.

I reply, "Well, that gambler lied to us."

The body and the car are dropped at the side of the road and we steal a parked Dodge minivan, loaded with a table, chairs, and a stereo.

"Look at the crowd. Hurry up!" Rick says.

💰

Agent Henderson is back at his desk in his office in Boston, which is fifteen by twenty feet with several files, a phone that has multiple lines, plus a computer. The phone rings. "Hello, this is Agent Henderson."

"Hi, I'm the local police chief, Chief Gibbs. There's been a jailbreak, and Tim and another man got away in a Mercedes."

"Thanks for the information. Do you have anything else?" asks Agent Henderson.

"Yes, sir. Two bodies have been found along with the Mercedes. There's no sign of any suspects."

"Thanks again for the information, Chief. I'll be in touch." Agent Henderson hangs up the phone and sorts through his notes.

"What a fine day," he says to himself.

The radio spills out another news report. "This is a special report. Police and federal authorities are on the lookout for Tim Masters, Rick Atkins, and Frank Zuccini. These criminals are considered very dangerous, so be careful. We have information on file on the FBI's website. If you have any information, please don't hesitate to call the authorities."

$

Tim, Rick, and I arrive in Vegas twenty-four hours later. It's full of casinos and hotels which light up the sky. It's hot and humid outside, but we manage to get a hotel using our Spanish names.

"Hey Mario," Tim says. "Why don't we get jobs as dealers?"

"Okay, Pedro and Jose, tell me all about it."

Rick says, "I have been here before, and there are marked cards that we use to screw the patrons out of their money."

There are cards in braille so I can do the job along with Tim and Rick. We get hired as dealers in the local casino, and things are going our way for a while.

"Look at that stash," Tim says, eyeing the money they had collected from patrons that was spread out on the table in front of them. It is supposed to go to the casino, but they have other plans.

Rick says, "Hey guys, we better get the stash and head back to the hotel. I think there're cops coming this way."

We hurry as fast as we can to our hotel loaded with a small bar.

"Do you think we got recognized?" I ask Rick.

"Let's pack up and get out of Vegas," suggests Tim before Rick can even answer.

"Relax. We need a little more money." Rick says.

"I knew something would go wrong," I tell them.

"Look, Frank, I'm tired like everybody else, but relax. We'll get by somehow," Rick reassures me.

$

Susanne, Peggy, and Jackie find a job at the cafeteria during their prison term.

"Well girls, we're going to make it," Jackie proclaims.

"Yeah, whatever," responds Susanne.

"I'll be glad to be outside these walls," Peggy adds.

The cafeteria is thirty-five by thirty-five feet with several tables, chairs, and a long counter for food service.

$

Agent Henderson gathers copies of his notes and sends them to Washington D.C. headquarters. The phone rings, and he picks up the receiver.

"Hello, this is Agent Henderson."

"This is headquarters. You're to fly to Vegas and interview the casinos because there's been trouble."

"Yes, sir, Mr. Christian," Agent Henderson answers. He ends the call and dials the number of the Chicago Police Department. John and Steve are at the office when they receive his call.

"Hello, this is John Schnyder."

"Hi, this is Agent Henderson. I was ordered to Vegas. We got a break on the three suspects."

John and Steve turn to Captain Edwards and tell him the news. "You're going to Vegas, gentlemen," he says.

"We'll meet you," John says to Agent Henderson.

"Sweet. I'll be at the Chicago airport."

Steve and John go to the airport to wait for Agent Henderson's plane.

"What you think, John?" asks Steve.

"We'll know more when we get there."

"My opinion is that there are other names involved," Steve says.

"There are no mention of names in the reports so far," responds John.

The plane Agent Henderson is on lands, and Steve and John board.

"Hi, fellas. Glad you can make it. I'll get more information after we get there," says Agent Henderson.

"Sweet," Steve answers. The three men ride together for the next few hours before they land in Vegas.

Tim, Rick, and I are at the hotel when the news comes on TV. "Good evening, everyone. This is a special report. We've discovered that Frank Zuccini and his companions are nearby. These men are considered very dangerous and will stop at nothing. We'll give more information as it becomes available."

"Okay, guys, you know we're famous now. Do you have any cop uniforms?" I ask.

Tim and Rick look through the clothes. "Here we are," says Tim.

"Whew. We'll get dressed like cops and get out of here," I say.

Rick replies, "Sweet. Let's go."

The three of us manage to get away as the crowd gathers to look for us. It's hot and humid and we're sweating inside the uniforms.

"Where do we go now, guys?" I ask.

"We go back to Peoria, Illinois. I've got family there," says Rick.

"No way. Peoria was bad luck for me," I object.

"We head back to Mexico. Those high-rise apartments are run by gangs," suggests Tim.

Steve, John, and Agent Henderson arrive in Las Vegas and rent an SUV which comes loaded with plush leather seats and a brand new stereo. Mr. Fred Doss, a man of five foot ten and 165 pounds, is waiting for them at the casino. "Hi, gentlemen. We've been expecting you," he says.

"Would you like to see the photos?" asks Steve.

"Yes, sir." Doss answers.

Steve hands him a copy of each criminal's photo.

"Now I recognize them. They used different names to work as dealers," Doss informs them.

"What were their names?" asks Agent Henderson.

"Their names were Mario, Jose, and Pedro."

"That helps out a lot. Is there anything else you can think of?" John asks.

"I thought something was weird because one of the men was blind. I didn't realize it's Frank and his friends until you showed me the pictures."

The phone rings while Doss and the policemen are meeting. He picks up the receiver. "Hello, this is Fred Doss."

"Tell the investigators we have a circus at the high-rise," a local policeman says.

"Let's go. We think the suspects are over there," says Agent Henderson.

"I'm glad to meet you gentlemen," Doss says. They shake hands before the FBI agent and the two policemen leave for the high-rise.

$

"We better hustle, Frank. There are cops coming," Tim warns.

Tim, Rick, and I hurry down the road in a stolen Chevy Malibu with Tim at the wheel.

"That was close!" I say.

"Get down, Frank!" Rick yells.

The car speeds past a road block where several shots are fired at them, breaking windows.

"Ouch! I'm hit! I'm hit! My head!" moans Rick while slumping in a heap like he was sawed in half.

"Wow, that's a lot of blood," says Tim.

"Rick! Rick!" I cry.

"It's no use, man. He died very quickly."

Tim keeps driving at 100 mph until the cops are out of sight.

"We're dumping the car and body here in the woods. We'll steal a truck and head back to Mexico," Tim says. I agree, but I'm feeling extremely depressed and paranoid. We drive through California in a 1997 pickup truck.

💰

Paul and Dorris visit Susanne, Peggy, and Jackie. They are led by a prison guard through the hall to their cells. The three women smile a little when Paul and Dorris come by.

"We are sorry and pray for you every day," Dorris says in tears.

Jackie replies, "We thought you gave up on us because you're Frank's brother and sister."

Susanne says, "We hope that Frank turns his life around. We should be getting out after half a year."

"We love you guys. Do you need anything?" Paul offers.

"Susanne and I need cigarettes and clothes," Peggy says.

Paul and Dorris promise them cigarettes and clothes when they come back for their next visit. Everyone shakes hands and huggs before the guard leads Paul and Dorris away. "Remember we pray for you guys," says Dorris.

When they are alone, Jackie says, "Well, girls, things are looking up, and we'll be out before Christmas."

Susanne and Peggy get excited. "That will be sweet!" Susanne says.

$

John and Steve receive a call from Captain Edwards while on the way to the high-rise.

"This is John."

"This is Captain Edwards. Do you have any information about where Frank and his friends are?"

"Hold on, Captain. We have more information."

Agent Henderson says, "John and Steve, I found out that a car and body were found. We believe it's Rick Atkins."

John says, "Captain, we'll text you the information."

The music on the radio is interrupted by the news. "Hello everyone, this is a special report. Local and federal authorities are intensifying their search for Frank Zuccini and Tim Masters. They're armed and dangerous, so be careful. Frank is visually impaired, and we want these criminals alive. Please contact the authorities via email and/or phone with any information."

"It looks like we're getting close," John comments.

Steve replies, "Frank and Tim are the only two left, unless they know some other family."

Agent Henderson's phone rings again. "Hello, Agent Henderson here."

"Agent Henderson, never mind how I got your number. You and the other cops are to stay away from Frank, or he will kill himself."

"Who is this?" asks Agent Henderson just as the phone goes dead.

$

Tim hangs up his phone. "Did you speak to the cops?" I ask.

"I got the guy who spoke to me while I was in prison and told him and the other cops better stay away or you'll take your own life. We're still going to Mexico, and we're going to relax on the beach."

"That sounds very good right now."

We drive through Arizona and Texas toward Mexico, and the weather gets hotter and more humid, with the temperature reaching above 100 degrees.

$

Steve and John are with Agent Henderson at the high-rise that the criminals had been staying in when the call was made to his phone.

"Who was that?" asks Steve.

"I recognized Tim Master's voice on the phone. He wanted to tell me and the other cops to stay away from Frank or he will take his own life." Agent Henderson breathes a sigh of disappointment. "We're done here at the high-rise, fellas."

The three men board a plane and head back to their respective offices.

$

Tim and I cross the Texas border into Mexico. We hear music and Tim slows to avoid all the people walking around. "Look at all the people," says Tim, rolling down the windows of an old Ranger pick up truck to let in the sounds of the people and music. The weather in Mexico is hot and humid.

"Let's get out of this festival." I say.

"Get down, Frank!" Tim whispers as he looks up to see a Spanish cop.

"Put your hands up, both of you," the cop says in English.

Tim draws his gun slowly and says, "Look, I have a present for your trouble," as a shot is fired from his gun, hitting the policeman in the forehead between the eyes. He falls backwards, facing up.

We hurry away from the crowd that is gathering and shouting, "There they are! It's them!"

The truck roars at 100 mph along the highway, with twists and turns jolting us.

"That was close, Tim."

"Trust me, Frank. We'll be okay."

Captain Rodriguez is looking through his notes and the phone rings. "Hello, this is Captain Rodriguez."

"This is Manuel," a shaky voice says. "My partner Miguel is dead."

"Where is he?"

"He is at the festival. A crowd saw two men leaving the scene. I think one is blind."

"Oh, no." says Captain Rodriguez.

The two policemen meet to file a report. Officer Manuel is a man of five foot eight and 190 pounds.

"I knew it," says Captain Rodriguez. "It's Frank and Tim back to start trouble. Can you describe them, Manuel?"

"One man was shorter than me, and the other man was taller."

Captain Rodriguez writes down the information and calls Agent Henderson.

"Hello, this is Agent Henderson. Can we help you?"

"This is Captain Rodriguez from Mexico. We need to talk because we suspect Frank Zuccini and his friend are back."

"What happened, Captain Rodriguez?"

"One of my officers was killed and the crowd saw two men riding away in a truck, but one was blind."

"I'll be in Mexico with a couple investigators to help in the search."

"That will be wonderful. We'll cooperate," Captain Rodriguez says.

Agent Henderson hangs up the phone, and immediately dials the number for Captain Edwards, who is eating his Ruben sandwich and orange when his phone rings. "Hello, this is Captain Edwards."

"This is Agent Henderson. We suspect that Frank Zuccini and his friend Tim are in Mexico."

"I'll get John and Steve to meet you, and we'll arrest these men."

John is eating pizza, and Steve is devouring a few tacos when Captain Edwards announces over the PA system, "Your attention! Will John and Steve come to my office?"

"It sounds like we've got something, Steve."

"It's time to move," agrees Steve. Both men finish their lunches and hurry to Captain Edwards's office.

"What's wrong, Captain?" Steve asks.

"Gentlemen, we have a break in the case. Frank and Tim are in Mexico, where you're to meet Agent Henderson and Captain Rodriguez. You will get more information there."

$

Tim and I are in an apartment complex listening to Spanish music on the radio when it is interrupted. "Good evening. We have late breaking news. Police and federal agents are still in a search for Frank Zuccini and Tim Masters. They were last seen leaving a festival where a cop was killed. If anyone is caught hiding these criminals, they will be arrested. Please, be careful; these criminals are dangerous, and you're urged to call the authorities if you know anything."

"Who cares," responds Tim. "Let's go eat tacos."

"The manager told us the restaurant was nearby."

We exit the apartment and get in the truck, but there is a crowd in our way of exiting the apartment area.

"Excuse us!" shouts Tim. The crowd begins chanting, "It's them! It's them!"

There are sirens and cops start gathering as we weave through the crowd and beep the horn.

$

Paul and Dorris are visiting in her home in Chicago, eating chicken-fried steak and potatoes for dinner when the phone rings.

"Hello, this is Dorris. Who's calling?"

"Hi, this is Agent Henderson of the FBI. I want to talk to the relatives of Frank Zuccini."

"I'm Dorris, and my brother Paul is here."

"Very good. We got a break in our search. Captains Daniels and Edwards told me it's okay to inform you that we have located Frank and his friend Tim in Mexico."

"Is Frank okay?" Paul asks from the extension.

"Yes, sir. He's very troubled, and we want to help your brother. Our hope is he'll turn himself into authorities."

Dorris replies, "We thank you for the information. Keep us informed of any further developments."

Dorris and Paul exchange goodbyes to the agent and hang up the phone.

"I don't know what to make of this, Paul." remarks Dorris. "Frank was always happy."

"Frank needs to get his life straight, but that may take years in prison."

The two finish their meal, and Paul says goodbye to his sister and heads back to Nebraska.

💰

Peggy, Susanne, and Jackie have finished their prison term, and are now being released on probation.

"Sweet! We've got our lives back," says Peggy.

It's a year later, and the investigation of Frank Zuccini continues while Jackie, Susanne, and Peggy begin their lives again. Jackie has a job working with kids at a day-care center.

Peggy has a job cleaning hotels, and Susanne is beginning a job as an employee at a hair supply store.

"I'm glad we moved to Nebraska," Jackie says.

"That's right, Mother. We're glad to get our lives back," replies Susanne.

Peggy adds, "I'm happy too."

💰

The air is sticky in Mexico, where Tim and I are still on the run.

"Let's rob that Tijuana bank," says Tim.

"Good idea. I'm sick of sitting around. Let's mogate."

We ditch the Ranger and steal a Plymouth coop. The ride takes about an hour, but we finally reach our destination.

"Be right back," Tim says. He walks into the bank with a note for the teller. It reads, "This is a holdup. Hand over money from all tellers, and no one will get hurt."

I'm alone in the car and don't realize that a crowd has gathered. Sirens are coming near and the door jerks open.

"That was close. I better make it quick," Tim says, sitting down and taking off.

I sigh with relief. "I was worried because a crowd had gathered and I didn't know where you were."

The car roars, and Tim turns and twists to avoid the cops and people.

"I'm sorry I left you alone, Frank, but that won't happen again. We almost got caught."

💰

Steve, John, and Agent Henderson stare at each other outside of the bank.

"Dammit! We almost had them," Steve says angrily.

John replies, "Calm down, Steve. We'll get them one of these times."

"It's up to the Mexican government to help us now," Agent Henderson says.

The three policemen, with the help of the Mexican police, interview everyone involved in the bank robbery.

💰

After the witnesses have been interviewed, John, Steve, and Agent Henderson meet with Captain Rodriguez at his office.

"I'm glad to have you gentlemen for help. Would you like some coffee?" he asks.

The three policemen nod their heads yes.

Captain Rodriguez pours cups of coffee and hands them out.

"Thank you," Agent Henderson says.

"Now, gentlemen, we were so close to the criminals. You have any more information about the Tijuana bank?" asks Captain Rodriguez.

Agent Henderson replies, "What we know is that one of the suspects entered with a note saying, 'This is a holdup. Hand over money from all tellers, and no one will get hurt.'"

"That's correct, and we interviewed witnesses in the area," John adds.

"Do you have a copy of the note?" asks Captain Rodriguez.

"Here are copies of the interviews and the original note." Steve says, handing them to him.

Captain Rodriguez opens his mouth to ask about the next plan when the phone interrupts him.

"Hello, Captain. This is Manuel. Have you located who killed my partner?"

"Manuel, we have some investigators from the U.S. helping us. They know who killed Miguel."

"Thank you, Captain. I'm sorry I had to tell his wife and children the bad news."

Captain Rodriguez hangs up the phone and says, "That was Manuel. I forgot to tell you the funeral for Miguel is tomorrow."

"It's all right, Captain," Agent Henderson says. "We'll be there."

$

The search continues as Tim and I hide out in a Mexican high-rise. "What will we do now?" I ask.

Tim thinks slowly. "We better lay low for a bit, Frank. We're on the most wanted list and could be headed to jail when we're caught."

I'm still worried, paranoid, and depressed inside. "Oh man, I hope we'll be okay."

"Frank, it's okay."

"Let's turn ourselves in." I suggest.

Tim jumps up. "We don't need that kind of talk, and you're crazy to think that the cops and prosecutors will let you off. I'll talk to you later!"

He storms into the bedroom and throws his clothes in anger on the floor as I sit on the couch and listen to Spanish music.

The next day the weather is hot and muggy, and Tim hasn't said a word since last night.

"Thanks for nothing, Frank. You got us into this mess," Tim finally says.

"Do you hear anything?" I ask him.

"Look, man, I should leave you here," he says, looking out the window in disgust.

"Hey, I'm sorry for mentioning turning ourselves in." I say, trying to ease the situation. "There is a noise outside."

Tim looks out the window again, and a shot comes through, whizzing past his head. "Get down, Frank!"

There at the window is a female bandit. "I want your money," she yells in Spanish.

"Don't make me hurt you lady," Tim shouts back.

"I don't understand," she says in Spanish.

I tell her that Tim will hurt her if she doesn't go away, but she refuses.

"Look, Tim, maybe she can help us," I say.

Tim fires a shot through the window, "Get in here!" he shouts.

She makes her way into the apartment. "You're to help us now," I tell her in Spanish.

Tim holds up his gun and says, "Be careful, Frank. I don't trust her."

She is five foot two, 135 pounds, and wearing a red blouse and red shorts down to her knees. The girl stands motionless for a few minutes. "You won't go to the cops?" she asks.

"Look, lady, you're to help us move along and be our driver." Tim says.

"Tim, I apologize for getting you mad," I say. He puts his arm around me and tells me that it's all right and not to worry. "I think the girl will be good," he concludes.

The woman, Tim, and I sit in the apartment talking for a while, and find out that the woman's name is Sandra.

"What's our next plan?" asks Tim.

"Sandra is our getaway driver after we rob a bank and steal a plane for London, England," I tell him.

Sandra smiles and says, "That will be sweet."

We leave the apartment and head for Cancun. "Be ready for when we get away," Tim tells Sandra.

We reach the bank location after an hour of driving and get out of the car. "Be careful, Frank. We don't have much time," says Tim.

We enter the building, and Tim pulls out his gun and a note which reads: "Hand over money from tellers or we start shooting." The crowd freezes as the money is handed out to Tim and me. One teller shouts, "They're here!" and Tim fires a shot. The bullet hits the teller in the right shoulder, and he falls back wincing in pain.

Tim says, "Anyone else want to be stupid?" The customers rush out quietly, and we hurry back toward the car. The crowd and the police gather as Sandra drives the car away.

"We're off to the airport near the border," says Tim.

"That was a close one," Sandra comments.

We get to the airport in Tijuana near the border and get out of the car.

"Let's go," says Tim as we enter the building. "We need a plane and pilot quickly!" he shouts to the manager. "If you call security, we'll shoot."

"Calm down, mister. It'll be all right," says Mr. Parr. "We'll do what you want. Tony, you're to fly these people where ever they need to go."

Tony is calm and collected as he tells the manager, "Yes, sir."

💰

John, Steve, and Agent Henderson leave Captain Rodriguez's office to continue their investigation.

"We will check airports, bus stations, train stations, and cabs for any suspicious activity." says Agent Henderson.

Steve's cell phone rings. "Hello, this is Steve."

"This is the hospital. Your wife went into early labor and has given birth to a healthy baby boy." Steve thanks her and smiles as he hangs up his phone. "My wife Cindy gave birth to our first child named Steve."

"What is his weight?" asks John.

"Eight pounds, seven ounces, and he's twenty-one inches long."

"Congratulations, Steve," Agent Henderson says. The three policemen, with the help of Mexican police, inform airports and bus and train stations to be looking for any suspicious activity.

Country music begins playing from Agent Henderson's phone, and he answers it. "Hello, this is Agent Henderson."

"This is Captain Rodriguez. The president of the Cancun Bank informed us that they've been robbed and one of their employees is shot."

"We'll be there to meet you," says Agent Henderson. Steve, John, and Agent Henderson meet Captain Thomas Rodriguez to investigate the Cancun Bank.

They arrive at the bank, surrounded by police and rescue personnel, to interview the bank president. They exchange greetings and Agent Henderson asks, "Can you tell us the details of what happened?"

The bank president, a man of five foot eleven, in his early sixties, and 175 pounds, looks up and says, "I thank you guys for coming. There were two people that entered through the front door and handed the teller a note demanding money, and threatening to shoot."

"Can you describe any of them?" asks Steve.

The banker pauses a bit, then says, "One man was short and blind, maybe five foot four. I couldn't tell the hair color. The other was taller and guiding his friend. There was a Mexican girl waiting in the car according to my employee."

"What's his name? He'd like to talk to him?" asks Captain Rodriguez.

"His name is Juan Flores."

The four policemen look over their notes and thank the bank president. "You're a big help. Here are our cards so you can notify us for anything," says Captain Rodriguez.

They get up from their chairs around the table and leave for the hospital.

"Look it's raining," says Steve.

"It sure is," John adds. The storm is coming through the area, and the wind picks up a little. Captain Rodriguez's SUV has air conditioning blowing through it as they ride to their next location. They enter the hospital with the smell of alcohol, sanitation, and other medications flying at them.

"We're here to talk with Juan Flores," says Captain Rodriguez.

The receptionist is startled, "Who are you?" she asks.

"We're the police," replies Agent Henderson.

"I'm sorry, gentlemen. He is on the second floor," she says.

They find the elevator and reach the second floor. Juan is watching TV when the policemen enter the room. "Are you Juan Flores? I'm Captain Rodriguez, and these are three investigators from the U.S. here to help us locate who shot you."

"Yes I'm Juan Flores."

Agent Henderson asks, "Can you give any details about what happened during the robbery?"

Captain Rodriguez's phone rings during the interview. "Hello, this is Captain Rodriguez."

"This is the manager of the Tijuana airport. I have a plane and pilot kidnapped, leaving Mexico, and they didn't say where they're going."

Captain Rodriguez hands the phone to Agent Henderson. "This is FBI Agent Henderson. Stay calm, and we'll straighten out the situation."

"Thank you, sir." says Mr. Parr.

"Make sure you have another plane survey and follow where they go," Agent Henderson says. He gives the phone back to Captain Rodriguez and says, "We have a plane and pilot hijacked by our suspects. I told the manager to have another plane tailing to be sure that the pilot will be all right."

"Now, Mr. Flores, what happened?" asks Captain Rodriguez. Juan thinks for a moment, "Well, two men entered the bank with a note that instructed to give money from all tellers or they'd shoot. I recognized one of them, and like a fool I shouted, 'It's them!' And got shot."

"Can you describe the two men?" asks Steve.

"One was maybe five foot five, and the other was five foot ten. Both had brown hair, and one guy was blind."

Steve responds, "Frank Zuccini is one of our suspects. We thank you for your time and hope you get better soon."

John, Steve, Agent Henderson, and Captain Rodriguez wish Juan a speedy recovery and exit the hospital. Their next step is to continue their investigation at the Tijuana airport.

$

Sandra, Tim, and I board the plane, and Tony gets in position for takeoff. "No funny tricks, or you're dead," Tim threatens.

Tony stays calm and asks for clearance.

"We're going to England, and you're not to tell anyone, is that clear?" asks Tim.

Tony says, "That's fine. Whatever you want."

I sit near the window while the plane speeds down the runway for takeoff.

"How long before we enter London?" Tim asks Tony.

"We're to arrive in six hours."

Sandra is amazed by the travel. "Keep your gun on him," she isntructs in broken English.

$

John, Steve, Agent Henderson, and Captain Rodriguez arrive at the airport to meet with the manager, Mr. Parr. He's at his desk pouring over his notes and says, "Glad to meet you guys. We want Tony safe and sound."

"We're John Schnyder, Steve Davis, Agent Henderson, and Captain Rodriguez," Agent Henderson says, introducing everyone to the manager. "Can you tell us what happened?"

"There were three people that appeared and wanted a plane and pilot to leave the country."

"Is there a plane following the hijackers?" asks Rodriguez.

"Yes, sir, they have GPS systems on the planes to track where they go."

Steve asks, "Can you describe the three persons involved?"

Mr. Parr replies, "The visually impaired man was maybe five foot four with brown hair and brown eyes, and the other man was maybe five foot ten with red hair and brown eyes. The third person was a short Mexican girl."

The policemen write on their clipboards, and Agent Henderson says, "We'll be sure to rescue the pilot and catch these suspects."

They look on the computer screen at the six-passenger plane followed by the surveillance plane. "Do you have any idea where the plane is headed?" asks Agent Henderson.

Mr. Parr answers, "Joe, the pilot of the surveillance plane, told me that the hijacked plane is possibly headed to London, England."

The storm has past and the sun is beginning to peak through the clouds as the four policemen shake hands with the manager and head back to Rodriguez's office to compare notes. Steve, John, and Agent Henderson find that things are okay back home to continue their investigation.

"Joe, this is Captain Thomas Rodriguez of Mexico, and we have three American investigators with us.

"I see the plane is headed for England, and Tony seems all right," says Joe.

"This is Agent Henderson, and we'll contact the English authorities for any unusual activity."

$

Sandra, Tim, and I are still in the air, approaching the London airport.

"Look at that crowd," says Sandra, pointing to the numerous people gathered on the runway.

A special report interrupts the radio. "This is a special news flash. America's most wanted Frank Zuccini is being sought for various crimes. This man is extremely dangerous and visually impaired, along with two companions who are also extremely dangerous. Frank is five foot four and 185 pounds. Tim Masters is five foot ten and 190 pounds. The third person is a Mexican girl. If you have any information, please call the authorities."

"There we are, pilot. You told somebody we were coming," Tim says, flinging his fists at the man.

"Stop, Tim! You're making this more dangerous than it needs to be. We need him to land the plane." I shout.

Sandra successfully pulls Tim off the pilot. Tim sits down, continuing to hold his gun at the pilot.

The plane lands without a hitch, and Tony says that it's safe to leave the airport, but there is a big gathering of English authorities.

Tim leads the three of us out of the plane with his gun aimed.

"Everyone, calm down, and stop, all three of you!" shouts Lieutenant Josh Quincy, a lean, six foot man with dark hair and blue eyes.

Tim moves his finger to pull the trigger, but a policeman shoots his arm before he can release a bullet.

"Keep still." says Lieutenant Quincy as he approaches us. "Well, we have been looking for a long time for you guys. I am Lieutenant Quincy of London. We have a big history with you guys. In fact, Tim, we know that you broke out of Boston Federal prison."

Tim, Sandra, and I are silent as the cuffs are wrapped around our wrists and an officer recites our Right to Silence. "You do not have to say anything, but it may harm your defence if you do not mention when questioned something which you later rely on in court. Anything you do say may be given in evidence." We're led away in police cars to the station where we are grilled for answers.

$

Steve, John, Agent Henderson, and Captain Rodriguez are in his office when the phone rings. He puts it on speaker phone and answers.

"This is Captain Rodriguez."

"I'm Lieutenant Quincy of England. We have three suspects in custody, and they're not talking."

Agent Henderson asks, "How are the pilot and the plane? Are they all right?"

"Yes, the pilot escaped injury, and the plane was allowed to go back to Mexico."

"Good. We're going to bring these people back to America and try them for their crimes," says Agent Henderson.

$

Tim has his arm patched up at the hospital, and is led back to the interrogation area where Sandra and I are in separate rooms being questioned.

"You know, Frank, we know that you're behind on your bills, but there's no excuse for these crimes," says Lieutenant Quincy.

I remain silent, and Lieutenant Quincy gives up on his interrogation. Tim, Sandra, and I are led back to our cells after none of us have cooperated in our questionings. "These suspects are to be sent back to America for trial," Lieutenant Quincy instructs.

$

The next day, Steve, John, and Agent Henderson shake hands and say goodbye to Captain Rodriguez before the three investigators depart to England to meet with authorities and arrange an interview with Tim, Sandra, and Frank Zuccini.

"Do you think they'll talk?" asks John.

Agent Henderson says, "No, that's why they need time away from each other."

John's phone rings as they're waiting for their flight. "Hello, this is John Schnyder."

"Congratulations, you guys. I got the call that the suspects are in England," Captain Edwards says.

"Thank you, sir."

He hangs up his phone and tells the others congratulations on behalf of Captain Edwards. They board the plane for London while outside the sun is shining through the clouds.

💰

Paul and Dorris are eating at Denny's enjoying eggs, bacon, sausage, and hash browns when his phone rings.

"Hello this is Paul."

"I'm calling because your brother is in England," says Captain Edwards.

Paul stops eating and gets a nervous look on his face as Dorris listens intently.

"What happened? Is he all right?" asks Paul.

"He didn't get hurt, but they shot his friend Tim because he tried to be a hero."

Paul's face shows relief, and he asks, "When do we get to see him? Is he talking?"

"No. Right now he refuses to talk, but we have Agent Henderson, John Schnyder, and Steve Davis flying to London to talk with authorities and arrange for their return to America for trial."

"Thank you so much, sir. You've done a fine job for me and Dorris over the past year." Paul hangs up his phone and says, "Thank God Frank is okay."

Dorris's face relaxed, and they finish breakfast.

"Well, Dorris, we've got to pray for Frank because the cops have them in custody in England."

"That's right, and hopefully he can straighten his life out," reminds Dorris.

They get into Paul's van and head back to Paul's house. It is late April, and there's a sunny sky in Nebraska with new leaves in the trees as a huge press conference is being set.

Agent Henderson, Steve, and John arrive in England to meet with authorities and decide to get a quick bite. They buy sandwiches and get in their rented car as Lieutenant Quincy waits to greet them. His office is aligned with plaques and awards of the English police department. Lieutenant Quincy is seated at his desk when a knock comes at the door.

"Who is it?" asks Lieutenant Quincy.

"Your secretary said you are here, and we've come to see you," says Agent Henderson through the door.

Lieutenant Quincy opens the door and invites the three American policemen to sit down at a round table for the interview. "Would you like coffee?" he asks.

The three investigators say yes, and coffee is served.

"This is John Schnyder, Steve Davis, and I am Agent Henderson of the U.S. We would like to arrange the trip for the suspects back to the States for the crime spree."

Lieutenant Quincy answers, "We were contacted by Captain Rodriguez of the Mexican government and that's why we were able to prevent any harm to their pilot. The suspects are not talking, but you gentlemen can see them shortly."

"What were the details of their capture?" asks Steve.

"Gentlemen, what happened was, after we received the call, we dressed some of our department to blend with the crowd at the airport." The story is interrupted by the phone ringing. "Hello, this is Lieutenant Quincy. Can we help you?"

"This is the warden. The Mexican girl is ready to talk."

Lieutenant Quincy thanks him for the information and hangs up the phone. "The rest of the story was that we waited until they got off the plane, and we shot one of the suspects because he pulled his gun."

John, Steve, and Agent Henderson look over their notes as they listen to Lieutenant Quincy. "By the way, the warden called and said the Mexican girl is ready to talk."

The fog is thick as the four policemen make their way from the office to the van. Their destination is London Maximum Security Prison where the Mexican girl, Sandra, is located in the women's division. She is waiting in her cell when the four men enter the building.

"Can we help you?" asks the guard.

Lieutenant Quincy replies, "I'm Lieutenant Quincy, and these men are from the U.S. We're here to interview the Mexican girl."

The guard buzzes the warden, who tells them to make their way to her cell.

Sandra is nervous in her cell when the four men reach the area. Her cell is nine feet by seven feet with a foam mattress.

Lieutenant Quincy says, "Young lady, we have three men from the U.S. here to talk to you. The warden told us you were ready to tell your story."

"I want to get out of here. My name is Sandra," she says in Spanish.

Agent Henderson says in Spanish, "You could get a lighter jail time if you testify against your two buddies. Tell us what happened when they picked you up."

"First of all, they forced me to go with them to rob a bank, then to the airport to come here to England."

Steve asks, "Why didn't you tell the police sooner?"

Sandra looks nervous and says, "They wouldn't believe me. I just want to go home."

Agent Henderson says, "Young lady, you will be traveling back to America, along with Tim and Frank Zuccini, and facing charges as the getaway driver. Were you forced to be with them?"

Sandra is growing angry and aggressive. "I told you yes. Why do you think I'm lying?"

Lieutenant Quincy replies, "Look, we are trying to find the truth, and you're making it difficult. You should have told us when we brought you here that you were not involved in this crime spree by choice."

John says, "We thank you and we're making arrangements."

The four policemen make their way over to meet with Tim Masters for an interview. Tim looks up with an emotionless face as the four policemen approached his cell.

"Hello, Tim. Remember me?" asks Agent Henderson.

"I am not talking. Get out of here!" Tim yells.

Lieutenant Quincy intervenes. "You know you're in a lot of trouble. You may not be eligible to be out of prison."

"Look, Tim, we know your history with Frank Zuccini. We have documented kidnapping, rape, murder, and robbery," says Steve.

John says, "The facts speak for themselves, and we also know about your escape."

Tim stays silent as the men look at their clipboards.

Agent Henderson says, "According to Sandra, you forced her to rob the Cancun bank and kidnap the pilot to bring you to England. Frank has a family to think about, but that could change because of the crime spree."

Tim starts throwing a fit as he pounds his fists into the mattress and shouts, "Get out of here! Get out of here!"

John, Steve, Agent Henderson, and Lieutenant Quincy move on to talk with Frank Zuccini.

I'm at the opposite end of the prison from Tim. The warden brings the four policemen to my cell. "Frank Zuccini, you have visitors."

"Hello, Frank. This is Lieutenant Quincy and these gentlemen are from the U.S. We're here to talk to you and arrange a trip back to the states."

I sit motionless, remembering thoughts about my family and job before this crime spree.

"Frank, you have set a bad example for visually impaired people. Your brother and sister are worried about you, and your ex-wife and her daughters have finally gotten their lives back." John tells me.

Agent Henderson says, "We have documented rape, murder, kidnapping, and robbery during this run. There is a way out of this Frank, if you're willing to testify against Tim and Sandra, who turned to us and claims that she was forced to do what you guys wanted."

I'm feeling overwhelmed and depressed, and I tell them I am not ready to talk.

Jackie, Susanne, and Peggy are in their living room watching a show when a special report interrupts their program.

"Good evening. I am Brian Wilcox of NBC news. We have breaking news that Frank Zuccini and his two friends have been caught. We have Captain Edwards of Chicago and Captain Daniels of Nebraska to answer any questions."

Flashbulbs click as Captain Edwards addresses the media.

"Good evening, ladies and gentlemen. We have caught up with Frank Zuccini, Tim Masters, and their newest accomplish, Sandra. They are presently in England with two of my investigators, who are working on arrangements for them to be flown back for trial."

Jackie sighs. "I'm glad that we've moved on." Peggy and Susanne nod their heads in agreement.

The press conference continues with a question about the details that led up to their capture. Captain Edwards speaks as the cameras click, "As you may have learned, the crime spree ran from Chicago, Illinois, to Omaha, Nebraska, Boston, Massachusetts, and Mexico. The FBI and our police forces have coordinated with the Mexican and English authorities to follow the plane and meet them at the airport." The crowd empties as the press finishes their conference by saying that if there are any more details the public will be informed.

$

John, Steve, Agent Henderson, and Lieutenant Quincy are informed of the press conference and arrange for the suspects to be flown back to the States.

"We think one will tell the truth, and there'll be separate trials," says Agent Henderson.

The three American policemen say their goodbyes with Lieutenant Quincy and head to the airport where the suspects are waiting to be transported. Everyone boards a military plane, and the suspects are shackled.

$

We arrive at the Chicago airport. Tim is still stone-faced and angry. I am depressed and worried; tears are running down my face because I know my family is concerned about the crime spree.

"Are you all right, Frank?" asks Steve.

I stand silent, and Steve continues, "Look, Frank, you're in deep unless you testify in court."

"Why do you care?" I ask.

The police drive us in their cars to Joliet Maximum Security Prison. I'm led by Steve, who tells me that his brother Jerry is blind, and works in Nebraska with Paul, my brother. The men then discuss the details of the trial. They have learned that a jury will be selected for each person's trial, and the trials will be held in Nebraska.

Agent Henderson says, "I'll testify if you need me. I'm going to head back to Boston since my job here is done."

Captain Edwards, John, and Steve shake hands with Agent Henderson and say goodbye.

$

Jackie's phone rings while Susanne and Peggy are doing their hair.

"Hello?"

"This is Luke Daniels, Captain of the Nebraska police. I've been informed to call you because Frank, Tim, and a Mexican girl named Sandra are back in Chicago."

Susanne and Peggy come over to their mother and listen intently. "We will be at each trial. Thank you for the call," says Jackie.

$

John, Steve, and Captain Edwards are looking over their notes from the investigation, knowing they need to bring their best points to trial. The phone rings, and Captain Edwards picks up the receiver. "Hello, this is Captain Edwards. Can we help you?"

Agent Henderson replies, "How are things? Are the suspects ready to give us information?"

"No. There's another press release scheduled for tomorrow to divulge the dates of each trial."

"Thank you. I'll keep an eye out for that." Agent Henderson says and hangs up the phone.

A press conference begins, and several investigators are there, including John, Steve, Captain Edwards, Agent Henderson, Captain Lucas from California, and Captain Daniels in Nebraska.

"Hello, everyone. This is Walter Kiper of CBS. We have details about separate trials for Tim, Frank, and Sandra. These suspects, as you know, went on a crime spree that started in Illinois, then took them to California, Vegas, and Mexico. There will be jurors selected for each trial to be held in Nebraska. We have Captain Lucas, Agent Henderson, Captain Daniels, and Captain Edwards to answer questions."

Captain Edwards comes up to speak. "I was made aware of the crime spree when we investigated the Holiday Inn in Chicago. Frank's ex-wife and two step-daughters have done their time, and are already working on getting their lives straightened out."

John and Steve come up next to speak. "Ladies and gentlemen, starting in May the first trial for Sandra Valdez will be in court," says Steve.

"That's right, Steve, and we have many details if anyone has any questions."

A question is asked by a reporter, "How is this different from any criminals in other cases?"

Steve replies, "This case is different because one of our suspects is visually impaired, but that doesn't make a difference. He is not above the law and should be accountable for his actions."

Captain Daniels comes up to address the media. "I learned about the crime spree because three ladies turned themselves in and said they're ready to face the consequences of what happened to them. They have straightened out, and their relationship with us is okay."

The press conference concludes and everyone leaves to prepare for the first trial.

$

Sandra is in court as May 10th has appeared. She is dressed in blue jeans, a T shirt, and tennis shoes. Her defense attorney, Shawn Sims, who is six feet tall with red hair, blue eyes, and wearing a gray suit with black shoes, begins saying, "Your honor, my client says that she was forced into the crime spree."

Matt Proctor is a man of five foot eleven with blond hair, blue eyes, and wearing a striped suit and brown dress shoes. He says, "The evidence shows that there was no forced intention, and she meant to leave from Mexico to England."

Judge Harold Nixon stands at six feet, and has black hair, brown eyes; he's wearing a white and black striped suit with black shoes. He says, "The case is number 15237. How do you plead, Mr. Sims?"

Sims answers, "Not guilty."

Judge Nixon says, "The trial is in two weeks on May 25th."

$

It is Monday, May 25th, the day of the trial for Sandra Valdez. Everyone is in court waiting for the trial to begin, including Lieutenant Josh Quincy and Captain Thomas Rodriguez. Jackie, Susanne, and Peggy are in the crowd as they watch Sandra approach the stage and sit.

"Order in the court," says the judge. "Everyone on the jury is not to talk to anyone about the case because of the publicity. I will begin with opening statements from each attorney, who will conduct themselves in a professional manner."

The crowd talks while Proctor stands up to speak. "Ladies and gentlemen, the woman you see is part of the crime spree. The evidence will no doubt show that she was not forced into action along with Frank Zuccini and Tim Masters. Her record is long in Mexico, and she was wanted for robbery before she left for England."

There is a whispering in the court room as Proctor steps back and Sims steps up. "Ladies and gentlemen of the jury, the evidence may show that the police are overstepping their boundaries in order to convict Valdez. She says she was forced at gunpoint by Frank Zuccini and Tim Masters to help them rob the Cancun Bank and hijack a plane for England because Tim and Frank were desperate."

Judge Nixon taps his gavel a few times as the courtroom crowd starts talking louder and louder. "Order in the court! The prosecution will start the proceedings, and the defense will have their say later on."

Proctor says, "The prosecution calls Captain Rodriguez."

Captain Rodriguez looks worn out as he makes his way to the podium.

Judge Nixon says, "Raise your right hand. Do you swear to tell nothing but the truth, sir?"

"Yes, Your Honor."

"State your name and occupation."

"I am Captain Thomas Rodriguez of the Mexican police and have twenty-five years' experience."

"How did you come across the defendant?" asks Proctor.

"She has a previous criminal record, and I believe she willingly followed Frank Zuccini and Tim Masters because Mr. Parr and the pilot, Tony, said she never objected to any of the action and didn't flinch at all when Tim held his gun to them."

"Is there anything you can tell us about before the plane was hijacked?"

"We talked with the president and an employee of the Cancun Bank, and Sandra, I mean the defendant, showed interest in what she was doing with Tim and Frank during the robbery."

"That's all," says Proctor.

Judge Nixon says, "Mr. Sims, do you have any questions?"

"Yes, Your Honor. Mr. Rodriguez, is it possible the she is telling the truth about being forced to do what she did, or is your mind swayed by the FBI and the local police investigating the case?"

Proctor exclaims, "Objection, Your Honor! The defense is reading more into the evidence being shown from the investigation."

"Sustained. Mr. Sims, rephrase the question."

"Captain, is it possible that she's telling the truth about being forced into robbing the bank and traveling to the airport?"

"No, it's not possible because she looked nervous when she talked to us about what happened."

Sims says, "That is all Your Honor."

"You may step down, Captain Rodriguez. Do you have any more witnesses?" Judge Nixon asks Proctor.

"Yes, Your Honor. The prosecution calls Tony, the pilot, to the stand."

Tony makes his way to the stage area.

"Raise your right hand. Do you swear to tell the truth so help you God?" asks Judge Nixon.

"Yes, Your Honor."

"State your name and occupation."

"I'm Tony Rivera, pilot at the Tijuana airport."

Sandra's face is fuming as Tony speaks. "You're dead!" she yells.

The courtroom erupts in gasps and whispers.

Judge Nixon bangs his gavel a few times, "Order! Order in the court! One more outburst and you'll be held in contempt!"

"What are the details of how you got to England, Mr. Rivera?" asks Proctor after the room has quieted.

"There were three people that entered the airport, and the defendant was one of them. She seemed nervous, but interested about what she was doing. They demanded for a plane and pilot to leave Mexico."

"Did they say where they wanted to go?"

"One person said they were going to England and not to tell anyone."

"Can you describe the suspects?"

"The defendant is here in the room," Tony says, pointing at Sandra. "The other two guys were arm in arm because one was blind. One man was maybe five foot ten, and the other man was five foot three with a cane and brown hair and blue eyes."

"That's all, Your Honor." Proctor says.

"Any questions for this witness, Mr. Sims?"

Sims begins, "Tony, you said the defendant seemed interested in what she was doing. Do you think it's possible that she was forced by the two men?"

"No, sir, she couldn't wait to get out of Mexico."

"That's all, Your Honor."

"You may step down, Tony, and good luck going back to Mexico," says Judge Nixon.

Tim and I are taken from Chicago by separate buses to Omaha. Tim is angry as John and Steve walk up to him in his cell.

"How are you, Tim? Are you sure you don't want to cooperate?" asks Steve.

"I knew it. Frank spilled everything! He's dead, I tell you. He's dead!" Tim yells as he stomps around the bed.

Steve's phone rings, and he answers. "Hello, this is Steve. What's up?"

"This is Captain Edwards. How are things going?"

"John and I are getting ready to interview Frank Zuccini because Tim needs counseling for his anger. He's thinking that Frank turned him in."

John watches Steve hang up his phone and asks, "Was that Captain Edwards?"

"Yes. He wants to know what's going on, and I said that Tim needs counseling."

John shakes his head and agrees with everything Steve is telling him.

💰

I'm sitting on my mattress as Steve and John appear at my cell door.

The guard says, "You have visitors, Frank Zuccini."

"Hello, Frank. This is Steve and John. How are you?" John asks.

"What's wrong with Tim? He won't talk to me."

"Look, Frank, he suspects you'll talk and wants to kill you, but now there's protection for you to talk about what's going on so you can straighten out your life," answers Steve.

I fidget with my hands while we are talking. "You guys are always starting something. I'm not ready to talk." I say.

"Frank, remember we'll be in court, and Agent Henderson will be here to see you while Sandra is on trial." John says.

"You can notify us when you get ready, Frank." says Steve.

Steve and John are led out by a guard as they leave the prison and head to their car.

💰

The courtroom is full while the trial is continuing.

"Order! Order in the court!" Judge Nixon asks the prosecution to call their next witness.

"The prosecution calls Lieutenant Josh Quincy from England to the stand," says Proctor.

Lieutenant Quincy comes out from the crowd and up to the stage area.

"Raise your right hand. Do you swear to tell the truth so help you God?"

"Yes, Your Honor."

"Please state your name and occupation."

"I'm Lieutenant Josh Quincy, Lieutenant of the English police department with forty years' experience. I've handled all types of people over the years."

"Mr. Quincy, do you think Sandra was forced by the other suspects to commit robbery and leave Mexico for England?" Proctor asks.

"No because Tony from Mexico reported to me, along with other interviews, that the defendant was very excited to be with the other suspects during this crime spree."

"We're sorry that you had to come all the way from England and wish you farewell." concludes Proctor.

"Do you have anything for this witness?" Judge Nixon asks Sims.

"Is it possible that you forced her into talking about being told to do the crimes committed?"

"No. The warden called us to say that she was ready to talk, and that's when she told us that she was forced by the other two men to rob the Cancun Bank and leave for England."

Sandra begins stomping her feet and screaming, "You're dead!"

Judge Nixon says, "Bailiff, remove the defendant from the courtroom!"

The police take Sandra back to her cell in the maximum security prison where she continues to be angry and violent.

Sims asks, "Mr. Quincy, are you aware that perjury could mean being prosecuted?"

"Yes, sir, that's why I researched the defendant's file and the other suspects' histories."

"That is all, Your Honor," says Sims.

"You can step down, Mr. Quincy, and have a safe trip back to England."

The crowd starts milling around in the courtroom while the judge looks over his notes and finally says, "This court is adjourned until tomorrow while the defense prepares its case."

💰

Agent Henderson returns to Nebraska to testify in court, when he arrives, he has dinner with Steve and John. Steve orders steak with mushrooms and onions, John has prime rib with radish sauce, and Agent Henderson has lemon-peppered chicken with garlic potatoes and vegetables.

"The food was delicious here at Bananza," Agent Henderson comments. "On another note, I have hair and DNA notes for you from the victims of our suspects."

"Thank you, Agent Henderson. We'll see you in court." says John.

John and Steve shake hands with Agent Henderson before they leave the parking lot of the restaurant.

§

Court is back in session the next day. Judge Nixon says, "The defense will start with witnesses, and Mr. Sims, you may begin."

"The defense calls on Fernando Valdez."

The crowd rumbles as the young man makes his way to the stage area.

"Raise your right hand, please. Do you swear to tell the truth so help you God?"

"Yes I do, Your Honor."

"Objection, Your Honor. The defense called the defendant's brother. He could bend the truth to protect her," says Proctor.

"Overruled. Please state your name and occupation for the record."

"I'm Fernando Valdez and work at a vegetable plant in Mexico."

"Mr. Valdez, what brings you here today?" asks Sims.

"Sandra told me that she was forced by the other two guys to rob the Cancun bank, where an employee was shot, and leave for England or she was killed."

"How often did you speak to your sister?"

"I talk to her every week, and she was sorry for her actions, but what was she to do in her position?"

"That's all, Your Honor," says Sims.

"Do you wish to cross examine this witness?" Judge Nixon asks Proctor.

"Mr. Valdez, is it true that you made up this story to save your sister's skin, and that you're wanted in Mexico for covering up for her?"

"No, sir, that's what she told me on the phone."

"Are you aware that we have witnesses to your sister's interest in the crime spree, and that perjury could mean jail time?"

"Mr. Valdez, you're to be taken into custody by authorities," Judge Nixon states.

The police arrest Mr. Valdez as he shouts, "Wait! Wait a minute!" He is driven to the Dunkin County Jail, and is awaiting trial for perjury.

"We're sorry for the delay, but we'll continue," Judge Nixon says.

Sims thinks for a moment. "I have no other witness and rest my case."

Judge Nixon taps his gavel a few times, then says, "Order in the court. The jury will hear closing statements from each lawyer and retreat to select a verdict."

Proctor says, "The evidence shows clearly that the defendant was interested in what she was doing, and there was no forcing her to rob the bank and leave for England. The pilot overheard her saying, 'Keep your gun on him.'"

Sims goes next and says, "Mr. Valdez was not lying about his sister, Frank Zucccini, and Tim Masters. The investigators have something to gain by saying that she was masterminding everything, but Frank and Tim led her on."

"We will adjourn and come back with a verdict in a few days." Judge Nixon concludes.

The courtroom empties with the crowd going in different directions.

$

Jackie, Peggy, and Susanne are watching TV when a knock is heard at the door.

"Who is it?" asks Jackie.

"Paul and Dorris," says Dorris.

Susanne opens the door. Dorris and Paul brought pictures of memories of the whole family, including Frank. They look over the photos during their visit and order pizza for dinner.

"What's wrong with Frank?" Jackie asks, getting upset.

"I talked with Agent Henderson on the phone the other day, but Frank refuses to talk," Paul says, shaking his head.

The sitcom that was on TV was interrupted. "Good evening, ladies and gentlemen. This is Brian Wilcox with a special update. The trial for Sandra Valdez of Mexico has reached the final phase. Stay tuned for a verdict and sentencing while her brother sits in jail for perjury."

"That explains everything," says Dorris.

Everyone gives hugs and kisses as they part ways back to their homes.

$

My thoughts are racing as I hear everything on TV; feelings of betrayal and distrust set in.

"Why is my life so bad?" I ask myself.

The guard calls my name as three men approach my cell.

"Frank Zuccini, you have visitors."

"Hi, Frank. This is Agent Henderson, John Schnyder, and Steve Davis. We're here to let you know that Jackie, Susanne, and Peggy are worried about you. Are you ready to testify against your friend Tim to get a lighter sentence?"

"No. I'm not ready because Tim is my friend."

"We'll be back if you need anything," says Agent Henderson after letting out a sigh.

The three policemen are led out by the guard, and I am back to sitting alone.

$

Proctor and Sims meet for lunch at the cafeteria in the courthouse. Proctor eats a hamburger with bacon, lettuce, tomato, onion, and mustard, while Sims has a couple tacos with lettuce, tomato, and hot sauce.

"You know the defendant is guilty with the evidence against her," Proctor argues.

"Yeah, I'm worried about her rights though and want to be sure that she's fairly treated by the process."

The two attorneys finish their lunches and head back to court.

"Order in the court," Judge Nixon demands. "Does the jury have a verdict?"

The foreman of the jury reads from the paper. "The jury finds Miss Sandra Valdez guilty of robbery, attempted murder, and kidnapping."

There are tears running down Sandra's face as she hears the verdict. "I'm sorry. I'm so sorry," she cries.

"We thank you for your service. Sentencing will be next month. Court is dismissed for the next trial."

John, Steve, and Agent Henderson leave with the rest of the crowd from the court while Sandra is led back to her cell.

"Look, it's sunny outside," says Steve.

"It certainly is nice," John adds.

"I hope you're ready to testify," says Agent Henderson, getting into his car to leave for the airport.

The policemen get in their van and start driving back to the office. The news comes on the radio. "Good afternoon, everyone. This is Marlin Layton with the local news special report. There has been a stabbing death at the women's division in the maximum security prison. The police have identified the body of Sandra Valdez, who was waiting on sentencing for robbery, attempted murder, and kidnapping. It was reported that she was fighting with another inmate and got stabbed with a knife in the chest. Frank Zuccini and Tim Masters are still waiting to be tried for their crimes. This is Marlin Layton with the special report."

💰

A press conference is scheduled for June 2nd, and everyone has gathered to hear an update.

"Good morning, everyone. This is Brian Wilcox with a special bulletin. Tim Masters, a friend of Frank Zuccini will be tried on Monday, June 9th, with Judge Nixon presiding. We have John Schnyder, Steve Davis, Captain Neal Edwards, and Agent Henderson to field questions and give details of any testimony. We thank you gentlemen for your service. Are there any questions?"

"John and Steve, how are Frank Zuccini and Tim Masters handling their situation now that they're locked up?" asks a front row reporter.

"The answer is Frank is refusing to talk while Tim thinks that Frank turned against him. We currently have Tim Masters in counseling for his anger," answers Steve.

"What makes this case different from any other criminal cases? Is it because Frank is blind, or should that be a problem?" asks a reporter from the back.

"No, it shouldn't matter that Frank is blind. He should be treated like any other person that breaks the law," says Captain Edwards.

"Would you have done anything different before the arrest of these criminals during the crime spree?" asks a third journalist.

"We did everything possible to the best of our ability. We got hair samples and DNA off of the victims, and the results are back from the lab to link these criminals," says Agent Henderson.

"We thank you gentlemen and want to thank Captain Rodriguez of Mexico and Lieutenant Quincy of England for their cooperation in this matter. This is good night from Omaha, Nebraska." Brian Wilcox says.

$

It's Monday June 9th. Judge Nixon is in court at his bench. Fitzpatrick and Rose are in the crowd as Sims is appointed for the defense.

"Order in the court. This is case number 43795 with the state versus Tim Masters. How do you plead?" asks Judge Nixon.

"Not guilty on all counts, Your Honor." Sims answers. Tim fakes a concerned expression as he stands up, but Sims says, "It's okay, Tim. I'll handle everything. Don't worry."

Tim sits back down with his hands folded in front of him.

"Ladies and gentlemen of the jury, there is to be no discussion about this case to anyone outside this courtroom and no bias of any kind. The process will begin with opening statements from each attorney and presentation of witnesses."

Proctor stands to speak. "Ladies and gentlemen, the evidence you will see paints the defendant as a hateful person who shows no remorse for his actions. We hope that you're fair in convicting this man so he pays for his mistakes behind bars for the rest of his life."

Sims stands next. "Ladies and gentlemen, the evidence you will see will describe the defendant as down on his luck and trying to find work, but it hasn't been the best of times. He was caught up with his friend, Frank Zuccini, who was behind on his bills and trying to make ends meet."

The crowd talks amongst themselves as Proctor and Sims go back to their chairs, but Judge Nixon taps his gavel. "Order in the court! Do you have your first witness, Mr. Proctor?"

"The prosecution calls John Schnyder to the stage area."

John walks up to the area in front of Judge Nixon.

"Raise your right hand. Do you swear to tell the truth and nothing but the truth?"

"Yes, Your Honor."

"State your name for the record."

"I am John Schnyder in robbery detail of the Chicago police, and an independent investigator assigned to cases involving criminals that start in Illinois and travel to other states."

"How did the defendant become involved in the crime spree with Frank Zuccini?" asks Proctor.

"He started at a convenient store down in East Peoria, Illinois, and then it moved to Nebraska, California, and Mexico."

"Do you have any questions about this man being part of the crimes committed?"

"No, sir. All the interviews point to the defendant here in court."

"How long has the defendant been friends with Frank Zuccini, Mr. Schnyder?"

"Our records show that the defendant went to high school with Mr. Zuccini and was alleged to drive the family out of Chicago after the hotel robbery."

"That's all, Your Honor," says Proctor.

"Are you ready to cross-examine, Mr. Sims?" asks Judge Nixon.

"Yes, Your Honor. Mr. Schnyder, you said that high school is where the friendship began, correct?

"That's correct."

"Well the defendant is angry because he believes his old friend has turned on him to strike a deal. Has his friend talked to you with details about the crimes?"

"No, sir. Frank Zuccini refuses to talk because he still thinks the defendant is a dear friend."

"Is it true that you guys are paying Frank Zuccini to testify against the defendant?"

"Objection, Your Honor. That's a false allegation," says Proctor.

"Sustained. Rephrase the question, Mr. Sims."

"Is there a reason the defendant would say that his friend turned against him?"

"No, sir. We've attempted to interview several times, but Frank Zuccini refuses to say anything about the crimes."

"That's a lie! That's a lie! I overheard the cops talk about money to get my friend to testify!" yells Tim.

"Order! The court will come to order! Mr. Masters, one more outburst and you will be removed from the courtroom!" Judge Nixon booms.

The crowd settles as the trial continues.

"Sidebar, gentlemen," says Judge Nixon.

Proctor and Sims gather near Judge Nixon.

"Mr. Sims, you are to keep your client restrained, and no money is being paid for testimony." Judge Nixon states.

The two lawyers go back to their respective chairs, and Sims says, "I have no other questions, Your Honor."

"You may step down, Mr. Schnyder." Judge Nixon instructs.

I'm alone in my cell when the warden says, "Frank Zuccini, you have visitors."

There at my door stand Jackie, Susanne, and Peggy. "Hello, Frank. We thought we could drop by to see you. How are you doing?" asks Jackie.

"Why do you care? You left me on my own when you took off for Nebraska."

"Don't go there, Frank. We did our time and got our lives back. We're concerned and hope that you will straighten out your life."

"Let's go, Mother," Peggy says as Susanne nods in agreement. The women are led out by the guard and don't say anything more as I'm left alone.

$

Judge Nixon looks at the clock on the wall and says, "This court is in recess until tomorrow with more testimony."

The crowd files out with Steve, John, and Captain Edwards meeting for dinner. Rose, Fitzpatrick, Sims, and Proctor go back to their offices to look over their notes. The four lawyers talk about their lives to take the stress off of work. They learn that Proctor has a wife and two young children, ages nine and ten. Rose is married with three children ages eleven, nine, and three years old, while Sims is a bachelor who is still looking for the right woman.

$

Tim Masters is back in court the next day when the trial starts.

"Order!" The court is back in session with Judge Nixon presiding. "Do you have other witnesses, Mr. Proctor?"

"Yes I do, Your Honor. The prosecution calls Maria Valdez to the stand."

The crowd moans, and Sims says, "Objection, Your Honor. She is the sister of Sandra Valdez who was killed!"

"Overruled. There is no relation between the two women. Please proceed."

Maria comes out from the crowd and up to the stage area.

"Please raise your right hand. The testimony you are about to give is the truth so help you God?"

Maria glares at the defendant and says, "Yes, Your Honor. I'm ready."

"State your name and where you work."

"I'm Maria Valdez. I work at a grocery store and volunteer to help the hungry."

"Can you tell us the details about the kidnapping and why you were picked?" asks Proctor.

"I was picked at random because I was thought to be pretty by four men running away. They threw me into the SUV, and the guy raped me and told me they need help across the border. Then they threw me out when they got in to Mexico."

"You were lucky because there's been several murders during this crime spree. How are you after your ordeal?"

"I'm getting help with counseling and great support from family."

"Can you point him out?"

Maria points her finger toward Tim, and with tears running down her face, she says, "He is right there."

Tim glares back and says, "You stupid girl! You're dead!"

Judge Nixon bangs his gavel a few times. "The court will come to order! Bailiff remove the defendant."

Tim is subdued and led out by the bailiff. He is then transported back to his cell at the maximum security prison.

"Sorry for the delay, but we'll continue the proceedings," says Judge Nixon.

"That is all," Proctor states.

"Are you ready to cross examine?" Judge Nixon asks Sims.

"Is it possible that you were willing to be with the defendant in that position?"

"Objection, Your Honor. That question should be stricken from the record because she's been through a lot," Proctor yells.

"Sustained. Rephrase the question, Mr. Sims."

"Miss Valdez, is it possible that you led him on?"

"No, sir. He forced himself on me, and I tried to get away."

"That's all, Your Honor," says Sims.

"You can step down, Miss Valdez. Will the prosecution call their next witness?"

"We would like Steve Davis to the stand," says Proctor.

Steve makes his way to the stage area.

"State your name and occupation."

"I'm Steve Davis of the Chicago robbery detail, and I have been there for fifteen years."

"The testimony you are about to give is the truth so help you God?"

"Yes, Your Honor."

"Mr. Davis, can you give details about everything that happened during this crime spree, and what led up to the defendant being captured?" asks Proctor.

"We'll begin with a convenient store robbery in which a car was seized. Then onto Mexico where a fight took place between the defendant and his friends against two Mexican bandits, who were found dead along with a man named George Powel. We met FBI Agent Henderson who compiled other evidence along with DNA results and hair samples."

"Ladies and gentlemen, we have copies given to the prosecution and defense of notes gathered by the local and federal authorities." says Judge Nixon.

"Mr. Davis, what makes this case unique from any other case?" asks Proctor.

"This case is different because the defendant's friend is blind, but it shouldn't matter; no one is above the law."

"According to previous testimony, the defendant is linked to a jailbreak and the bodies of a gambler and inmate were found. Is that right?"

"Agent Henderson phoned us the news of the defendant's capture and later break out with another inmate. He then headed to Vegas, but two bodies and the car were found near the highway."

"That's all, Your Honor," says Proctor.

"Do you have questions, Mr. Sims?"

"Yes, Your Honor. Mr. Davis, is it possible that evidence was planted to frame this man?"

"Objection, Your Honor. That's all distorted," says Proctor.

"Sustained. Rephrase the question, Mr. Sims."

"I withdraw the question. Mr. Davis, is it possible that Frank Zuccini had something to do with the defendant's anger?"

"Frank refuses to talk, but it's possible that he said something to the defendant."

"I hope that you don't feel sorry because the defendant's friend is blind. Do you?" asks Sims.

"Objection, Your Honor! The defense is badgering the witness," Proctor exclaims.

"Overruled. You may answer the question, Mr. Davis."

"I talked with Frank about the fact that my brother Jerry is blind, and blind persons don't feel sorry for themselves, nor do they expect anyone to feel sorry for them. The defendant and Frank Zuccini are not above the law."

"Have you planted evidence to convict my client?" asks Sims.

"Objection. That is false, Your Honor," says Proctor.

"Mr. Sims, that question will be stricken from the record because there is no sign of evidence tampering."

"That is all, Your Honor," says Sims.

"You can step down, Mr. Davis. The court is adjourned for lunch."

Several people head down to the cafeteria, including Steve, John, Agent Henderson from Boston, and Captain Edwards.

"What a beautiful day outside, and Nebraska is laid back," Agent Henderson comments. The weather is around 80 degrees outside.

"That is right, Robert, and the hunting isn't bad," laughs Edwards.

"That sounds good. We had better get back though," says John.

The four men eat their sandwiches quickly and head back to the auditorium for the trial.

"Order." says Judge Nixon while the crowd settles into their seats. "Does the prosecution have any more witnesses?"

Proctor looks at his list, "Agent Robert Henderson."

Agent Henderson makes his way to the stage.

"State your name and occupation please."

"I'm Agent Robert Henderson with the FBI and I've been with them for twenty-five years. My experience before was with the Boston police department for ten years."

"How did you become aware of the defendant?" asks Proctor.

"My involvement started because I met the defendant at the federal prison, and my notes show he had a history before he got there."

"Do you have any doubt as to the link the defendant has with the victims in this case?"

"No, because I brought back the hair and DNA results from the lab that indicate the defendant at the scene of each crime."

"Thank you, Your Honor," Proctor concludes.

"Do you have any questions, Mr. Sims?" asks Judge Nixon.

"Agent Henderson, is it possible that there could be a mistake with the results?" asks Sims.

"Objection, Your Honor. The defense is saying that the evidence is tampered." Proctor says.

"Overruled. Answer the question, Agent Henderson."

"The results matched the defendant sir."

"That's all, Your Honor," says Sims.

"You can step down, Agent Henderson."

Proctor says, "The prosecution rests its case, Your Honor. Mr. Quincy and Mr. Rodriguez have previously testified."

Judge Nixon asks, "Does the defense have any witnesses?"

"Will Mrs. Dan Masters come to the stand?"

The crowd whispers as Tim's mother makes her way to the stage area.

"What happened with my boy? He's not here!" shouts Mrs. Masters.

"Calm down, ma'am. He's back at the jail because he was in contempt," Judge Nixon reassures her. "State your name and occupation."

"I'm a nurse from Illinois where Tim, I mean the defendant, grew up. He's always been in with the bad crowd, but I'm here to support him."

"What makes you believe he's innocent?" asks Sims.

"This is the first time I heard about him when the news began, but I thought he was smarter than that."

"How was his childhood?"

"He was always adventurous and played with other children in the neighborhood where he and Frank Zuccini grew up."

"Thank you, Mrs. Masters," says Sims.

"Mrs. Masters, you said he was always in with the bad crowd. What did you mean?" interjects Proctor.

"I mean the kids were always in trouble, and we wanted Tim not to hang with them because he would be in trouble with the law," Mrs. Masters answers.

"Is his father in the picture?"

"No. Tim's father died in an automobile accident when Tim was nine, and I never remarried."

"That's all, and thank you, Mrs. Masters. You are free to go," says Judge Nixon.

"I rest my case and have no other witnesses Your Honor," says Sims.

"Ladies and gentlemen of the jury, there will be closing statements before a verdict can be done. The jury will be secluded for a while," says Judge Nixon.

Proctor gets up to speak. "Ladies and gentlemen, the photos and testimony of witnesses clearly state the guilt of the defendant, and one victim has identified him as a suspect. I hope that you're fair in the conviction that will put him away for a long time."

Sims gets up to speak after Proctor sits down. "Ladies and gentlemen, I think there could be a mistake in the evidence that links this man to the crimes. He is angry with his friend Frank Zuccini, and we need to find out because he may have been pushed by Frank to commit these crimes. I hope that you're fair in letting this man free on lack of evidence."

Judge Nixon concludes, "This court is adjourned, and a verdict will be reached in a few days."

The courtroom empties with the crowd heading toward the area in which a press conference is being held.

"Good evening, ladies and gentlemen. This is Brian Wilcox of NBC. We know so far that the alleged friend of Frank Zuccini is waiting for a verdict. Stay tuned for more details as they become available."

"Wow what a scene," Benny says to Christine.

"That's wild. I'm glad we've moved on," says Susanne. Jackie, Peggy, and Susanne are visiting Benny and Christine in their new home, complete with two bathrooms, four bedrooms, and a fireplace. Their living room has a forty-two-inch plasma flat screen TV, a computer, and a stereo with speakers surrounding the area.

The cameras click as everyone was watching on TV. "Good night from Omaha," says Brian Wilcox as the press leaves for their offices.

$

It's June 17th when the verdict is available.

"Foreman of the jury, have you reached a verdict?" asks Judge Nixon.

The foreman reads the paper as each juror had agreed to, "Guilty on all counts." It is tense as Tim Masters hears the news.

"Will the defendant please rise and remain standing? Sentencing will be next month, and court is adjourned. We thank you for your service," Judge Nixon says to the jury memebers.

The courtroom empties with Tim's mother and the crowd going in different directions, waiting for sentencing and a new trial for Frank Zuccini.

I'm still alone as the guard comes by the door. "Frank Zuccini, you have a visitor."

"Hello, Frank. I'm your defense attorney. My name is Travis Fitzpatrick, and I've been appointed to represent you in trial."

I think for a moment before saying, "I'm sorry for what I did, Travis, but what can I do to make it right?"

"Look, Frank, your friend Tim thinks you turned him in to the authorities after you guys were picked up at the London airport, and he wants you killed. My advice is to testify at sentencing, and you should get a lighter break."

"What if I told you that Tim is my friend?" I ask.

"Yes, Frank, but if you want to spend the rest of your life behind bars I wouldn't call that friendship because he wants you dead."

"I'll see you later," I say as Travis shakes my hand and leaves my cell. My thoughts are racing the next day when Warden Stevens comes by my cell door.

"Let's go, Frank. You're to be in court for the sentencing of your friend and your hearing for trial."

The weather outside is warm, and I can feel the breeze on my face as I'm led in cuffs to the bus for transportation.

There is a big crowd outside the courthouse as I am brought before Judge Nixon. "Hello, Frank. Be seated and wait," he instructs.

I am led to a chair near Steve.

"Order in the court! Will the defendant please rise and remain standing? The jury of your peers has found you guilty of murder, kidnapping, robbery, and sexual assault. The sentence placed on you is life in prison with no parole for twenty-five years because the crimes are severe."

Tim glares at the judge, then sees me and yells, "You're dead, Frank!"

I stand up to speak. "Your honor, I realize the consequences of my actions, and my friend needs counseling for his anger. I said we should turn ourselves in, but I told him I was sorry."

The crowd starts chattering as Judge Nixon bangs his gavel. "The court will come to order. Please take the defendant out while we continue on with the next case."

Everyone in court quiets down as Judge Nixon looks over his notes. "Will the next defendant please rise?"

I stand as Judge Nixon says, "This is case number 53797 with the state of Nebraska versus Frank Zuccini. How do you plead?"

"Not guilty, Your Honor," says Travis.

"Frank, your trial will start next month around August 12th, and court is adjourned."

$

"This is Marlin Layton of the local news. Frank Zuccini appears before a grand jury to start trial for a crime spree that spread throughout the country. There are limited details because of the publicity, and we have Captain Edwards of Chicago and Captain Daniels of Omaha to field questions."

The cameras click as a reporter asks, "How does Frank feel now that he's been caught, and isn't he setting a bad example for people with disabilities?"

Captain Edwards replies, "Yes, he is setting a bad example, and is remorseful for his actions according to his lawyer. Frank realizes that things will get better, and knows he is not above the law."

"If there are no more questions, we thank you for coming. This is Marlin Layton from Omaha, and good night." Everyone left as the media concluded its newscast.

I'm brought into court to begin trial for my role with the crime spree.

"Order in the court. This is standard procedure that we begin with opening statements of the prosecution and defense. There is to be no talking to the media about this case and no cameras allowed during all the testimonies. The attorneys will conduct themselves in a professional manner. Let's begin the proceedings."

Proctor gets up to speak. "Ladies and gentlemen, the evidence from the crime spree will show the affect the defendant Frank Zuccini had on the lives of the people encountered during said crime spree. He has no vision, but that shouldn't matter in this case because the defendant should pay for his role. The evidence will prove his guilt, and I ask for your fairness in convicting this man to serve time in jail for the rest of his life."

Proctor sits down as Fitzpatrick stands up to speak. "Ladies and gentlemen, there is evidence to support that the defendant, Frank Zuccini, was pushed into crime because of bad luck and pressure in trying to support a family on little money. He realizes the consequences of his actions and wants to make it right for himself, so he can set a better example for others with disabilities to stay away from crime because it's not worth the trouble. We hope that the testimonies will fairly show that Frank is sorry and intends to straighten out his life."

"Thank you, gentlemen. Does the prosecution have their first witness?" asks Judge Nixon.

Proctor replies, "We call Dave Anderson to the stand."

Dave walks up to the stage in front of Judge Nixon.

"Raise your right hand. The testimony you're to give is the truth so help you God?"

"Yes, Your Honor."

"Mr. Anderson, is this the man that was at the hotel when it was robbed?" asks Proctor.

"Yes, he was the one in back of the line when they made their appearance."

"Can you tell us what happened during the robbery?"

"There were four people that entered the vault area and said they had valuables. They said to make it quick. The defendant carried a cane, and that's how I knew he was blind."

"Is there anything else you can tell us, Mr. Anderson?"

"No."

"That is all, Your Honor," says Proctor.

"Mr. Anderson, you seem sure of yourself now, but in your previous testimony you weren't so sure if there were two or three ladies with the man described above. Are you sure that this man was in the area?" asks Fitzpatrick.

"Objection, Your Honor. The defense is badgering the witness," Proctor argues.

"Overruled. Answer the question, Mr. Anderson."

"I wasn't sure because I was concerned about my safety during the ordeal, and that's why I asked my coworker Mike to help me."

"You were intimidated by the fact that the defendant is blind and wanted to feel sorry for him, is that right?" asks Fitzpatrick.

"Objection, Your Honor. The defense is trying to make blindness an issue, and the previous testimony has nothing to do with this case."

"Sustained, and sidebar, gentlemen."

The two lawyers argue as they approach the bench.

"Gentlemen, you are to conduct yourselves according to business. Let's continue because the defendant's disability won't be an issue," says Judge Nixon.

Proctor and Fitzpatrick go back to their respective chairs while Dave Anderson waits patiently.

"I withdraw the question, and that's all Your Honor," says Fitzpatrick.

"Thank you, and step down, Mr. Anderson," says Judge Nixon.

"The prosecution calls Lieutenant Sorrenson from Peoria, Illinois, to the stand," says Proctor.

Mr. Sorrenson makes his way to the stage area while I sit and listen to everything.

"Raise your right hand. The testimony you will give is the truth so help you God?"

"Yes, Your Honor."

"Mr. Sorrenson, you were interviewed by two investigators from Chicago about a convenient store robbery. Can you describe anyone and what happened at the scene?" asks Proctor.

"Yes, two men entered the store while there were two other fellas waiting in the car. The car roared away with all four men, and shots were fired that missed due to the rain."

"Can you point him out?"

Lieutenant Sorrenson points his finger toward Frank Zuccini and says, "That's him. He was waiting in the car during the robbery."

"That's all, Your Honor," says Proctor.

"Are you ready to cross-examine, Mr. Fitzpatrick?"

"Mr. Sorrenson, is it possible that evidence was planted to frame this man?" asks Fitzpatrick.

"Objection, Your Honor. There is no sign of evidence tampering," says Proctor.

"Sustained. Rephrase the question."

"Mr. Sorrenson, is it possible that this man is framed by the evidence against him?"

"No, because the evidence matched the defendant's hair and fingerprints."

"Why were shots fired? Because someone innocent could have gotten hurt," Fitzpatrick accusees.

"I admit, we could have handled the job better, but we thought we could slow down the car by shooting the tires."

"That's all, Your Honor." says Fitzpatrick.

"You can step down, Mr. Sorrenson."

The temperature outside the courtroom is 75 degrees with the wind gusting 15 mph. It's about noon when Judge Nixon says, "Court is now adjourned for lunch. Be back at one o'clock."

Everyone scatters as I am led back to my cell. "We'll be back, Frank," says the bus driver as he walks away. My head is feeling light because I'm going through withdraw from alcohol and marijuana that I have taken almost daily over the past few years.

A familiar voice nearby says, "Are you all right, Frank?"

I cry and say, "I'm sorry I messed up, Mom."

"Look, Frank, Paul, Dorris, and your dad, along with Jackie, Susanne, and Peggy are worried sick, and that's why I flew here to see you at lunch."

My thoughts race as my mom continues, "Steve Vickers is here for prayer guidance and would like to see you."

"When I get sentenced, Mom, send him anytime because I'm praying."

A guard leads my mother out of the building while I get back on the bus to the courthouse for the next session.

"Order in the court. Trial is ready to continue," says Judge Nixon.

"The prosecution calls Mr. Nick Drake to the stand," says Proctor.

I hear his name, and all my feelings about him begin swirling around my mind, but I'm ready to face whatever comes my way.

Mr. Drake makes his way up to the stage area.

"Raise your right hand please. Is the testimony you're to give the truth?"

"Yes, Your Honor."

"State your name and occupation, Mr. Drake."

"I'm Nick Drake, director of Business Enterprise Program for the blind."

"Mr. Drake how long were you at that position, and how many years did the defendant work for you?" asks Proctor.

"I have held the position for twenty years, sir, and the defendant has worked with us for seven years."

"Can you explain why he was kicked out, and why he went on the crime spree?"

"Frank was investigated by the program for stealing from all the machines and marking invoices paid when he actually took the money to keep up with his debts. Therefore we took inventory to remove him from the program. He didn't care at the time, and I hope there's help available for him to turn around his life."

"Mr. Drake, does this photo match the defendant in the room?" asks Proctor.

"Yes. The picture shows him and another man standing at the London airport."

"That's all, Your Honor," says Proctor.

"Are you ready to cross examine?" Judge Nixon asks, looking at Fitzpatrick.

"Are you aware that the defendant tried for help and didn't get a response?"

"That is not correct, sir. We've tried several times to help the defendant, but he refused saying that we ran his life too often."

"The defendant is here today because charges of murder, kidnapping, robbery, and sexual assault are against him. Don't you think that Frank needs another chance at life?" Fitzpatrick urges.

"Look, sir, I'm stunned like you because when I first met Frank, I didn't think he would resort to crime as a way out of financial problems, and I didn't expect murder to be part of the crime spree."

"That's all, Your Honor," says Fitzpatrick.

"Thank you, and step down, Mr. Drake," says Judge Nixon.

"Will Agent Henderson come to the stand?" asks Proctor.

Agent Henderson makes his way up to the stage area.

"Raise your right hand please. The testimony you're to give is nothing but the truth?"

"Yes, Your Honor."

"State your name and occupation."

"I'm Robert Henderson of the FBI, and I've been an agent for twenty years."

"Agent Henderson, can you explain how you met the defendant and how he matched the crimes committed during the spree?" asks Proctor.

"Yes, sir. I met his friend Tim while he was in prison, and after that, I met Frank in London, England, and he was refusing to talk to us. The crimes committed matched the DNA and hair samples from the lab along with the fingerprints."

"Agent Henderson, how do you see the defendant differently from any other criminal if any?"

"Objection, Your Honor. The prosecution is trying to bring up the issue of blindness," Mr. Fitzpatrick interjects.

"Sustained. Rephrase the question, Mr. Proctor."

"Agent Henderson, is there a difference between the defendant and other criminals you've dealt with in your experience?"

"Yes, sir, he's blind, but that doesn't matter in this case."

"Have you talked with the defendant since he came back to America?"

"Yes, sir, several times to check on him and to find out if he's ready to talk about what happened during the crime spree."

"That's all, Your Honor," says Proctor.

"Would you like to cross-examine, Mr. Fitzpatrick?" asks Judge Nixon.

"Agent Henderson, has there been a psychiatrist to examine Frank to make sure he's all right, given that this crime spree seems out of character for him?" Fitzpatrick begins.

"Objection, Your Honor. That is hearsay. Agent Henderson is independent from the prosecution," says Proctor.

"Sustained. The last question is struck from the record. Ask another question, Mr. Fitzpatrick."

"Agent Henderson, is it possible there's another chance at life for Frank because he was behind on his bills and mortgage?"

"Yes, it's possible because we've interviewed many times and he refuses to say anything about his friend and the crimes committed."

"Do you think that mistakes have been made with the results to take advantage of the defendant?"

"Objection, Your Honor. The defense is suggesting that the evidence is tampered," says Proctor.

"Sustained. Rephrase the question," orders Judge Nixon.

"Agent Henderson, is it possible that there are mistakes in the results because he feels he's unfairly treated?" asks Fitzpatrick.

"We have policies in place to ensure that mistakes are prevented, and the defendant is treated the same as everyone else, no matter that he's blind."

"That is all, Your Honor," says Fitzpatrick.

"Thank you. Step down, Agent Henderson. The court is adjourned until tomorrow."

All the people exit the courtroom. I can hear the news on the TV as I am led back to my cell.

"This is Marlin Layton with the special report. The maximum security prison is on lockdown after a fight was broken up between two inmates. One of the inmates appears badly beaten, and it doesn't look like he'll survive. He has been identified as Tim Masters. Mr. Stevens, can you tell us what happened?"

"The fight started over a baseball game, and Mr. Masters got very angry. Jared Hicks, the other inmate, retaliated and violently threw Tim on the ground. He then proceeded to beat repeatedly Tim in the head and torso with his fists." Warden Stevens says.

My body is numb with shock and disappointment. At this moment, I know I have to turn my life around.

"This is Marlin Layton with the special report. and goodbye for now."

The next day I am again brought back to court for the trial. I feel groggy from lack of sleep that night.

"Order in the court," says Judge Nixon with the crowd settling. "Does the prosecution have other witnesses?"

"We rest our case," says Proctor.

"Your honor, the defense needs more time to prepare witnesses," Fitzpatrick says.

Judge Nixon says, "More time is denied. Please continue the proceedings."

"The defense calls Mrs. Paul Zuccini to the stand."

I was relieved when my mother was being called to testify. Mary Zuccini makes her way up to the stage area with the crowd groaning.

"Order in the court. Raise your right hand. The testimony you will give is nothing but the truth?" asks Judge Nixon.

"Yes I do, Your Honor."

"State your name and occupation, Mrs. Zuccini."

"I work in the agriculture building in Chicago, and my name is Mary Engle Zuccini."

"Mrs. Zuccini, what was Frank's childhood like growing up?" asks Fitzpatrick.

"He was like any other boy. We raised him to be as independent as possible. He liked movies, sports, and heavy metal music, and he enjoyed learning Spanish. I was shocked when I found out the defendant was on the run because he started strong and became a successful vendor."

"Did you notice any signs that he would be a criminal?"

"Your honor, my son fell behind on his bills because he was only trying to support a family, and as far as I'm concerned, he needs another chance to make it."

"That's all, Your Honor," says Fitzpatrick.

"Are you ready to cross-examine?" Judge Nixon asks Proctor.

"Mrs. Zuccini, your son Paul testified that his brother needs to pay for his mistakes and straighten out his life. How did you feel about his testimony?"

"It's true about what Paul said, but we're all here to support Frank and his rehabilitation to turn his life around because I've talked with Frank and he understands that he has to deal with the consequences."

"The previous testimonies state that there's been no criminal record before the hotel robbery. Are you aware the defendant was stealing from the vending program for the blind?"

"I was not aware of that until Mr. Drake testified that indeed he stole from the vending program, and I'm hurt by those events."

"That's it, Your Honor," says Proctor.

"Thank you, Mrs. Zuccini. Step down please."

"We rest our case, Your Honor," Fitzpatrick says.

Judge Nixon looks over his notes while I sit listening and waiting.

The news comes on the TV after we adjourn for lunch. I listen as I am led back to my cell.

"Good afternoon, ladies and gentlemen, this is Brian Wilcox of NBC. The local newscast told of two inmates brawling over a baseball game, and one was identified as Tim Masters, a friend of Frank Zuccini, who is now on trial for his role in the crime spree. We were able to conclude that Tim Masters passed away due to his injuries sustained in the fight. The other inmate has since been transferred to another facility."

I am saddened by the loss. I am transported back to court for the next phase.

Judge Nixon taps his gavel. "The court will come to order. Ladies and gentlemen of the jury, it's now time for closing statements, and the evidence will be weighed for as long as need be."

I sit and listen as Proctor stands up to speak, "Ladies and gentlemen, the testimonies you have heard clearly show that the defendant intended to commit crimes, no matter that he is blind, and took advantage of the banks, stores, and the people that were killed along the way. This man should serve the rest of his life behind bars, and I hope that you're fair in the conviction because there's no doubt in what happened here."

"Stay calm, Frank. We'll handle everything," Rose says as he lays a hand on my shoulder. I lean back in my chair as Travis stands up to speak, "Ladies and gentlemen, the previous testimonies indicate the possibility that mistakes are made in the hair samples and DNA results. The defendant realizes that the drama of the crimes was not the answer to his money problems, even though his family was behind on their bills and mortgage. We hope that you're fair in examining the evidence and determine that he doesn't need the rest of his life behind bars. Frank wants rehabilitation so he can help others with disabilities to live in society."

I wait as Judge Nixon says, "Ladies and gentlemen, the jury will be secluded for a few days to examine the evidence, and court is now adjourned until a verdict."

My family gathers as everyone scatters in different directions from the courtroom. I cry as Dorris, Paul, my mom and dad, along with Jackie, Susanne and Peggy, give me hugs and say, "We love and miss you as part of the family."

A guard takes me back to my cell, where I am to wait until the verdict.

$

A week later I am brought back to court and wait anxiously as the verdict is read.

"Foreman of the jury, have you reached a verdict?" asks Judge Nixon.

The foreman looks over his notes and says, "He's found guilty of robbery, but not guilty of sexual assault and murder."

The crowd moans after the verdict is read, and Judge Nixon says, "We thank you for your service, ladies and gentlemen. The sentencing is next month, Frank, and we hope that you've learned a huge lesson in the law."

I am led back to my cell by authorities to wait for sentencing. I pray for rehabilitation for a better life ahead.

$

I am brought back to court on September 12th for my sentencing.

"Order in the court," says Judge Nixon as the crowd waits impatiently. "Will the defendant please rise and remain standing? You have been found guilty by a jury of your peers, and will serve ten years in jail because robbery is severe. Your term will include prayer guidance by your local church, family therapy, and a job. This job may be putting toothpaste into boxes or packing toilet paper, and education is available."

There are tears in my eyes as I am led away to serve my jail time. A crowd has gathered around my jail cell as the news crew is setting up for a conference.

Fitzpatrick pauses then says, "I'm sorry. I tried for a lighter break, Frank, but I have confidence in your goals to get on with your life."

"This is Brian Wilcox of NBC with a special report. We're here with Frank Zuccini. Can you tell us what goals you have set for yourself while in jail?"

I take a deep breath and say, "My goal in jail is to help others, strengthen my spiritual guidance, do the best job at work, and update my computer skills to be marketable in society when I leave prison."

💰

My luck begins to change for the better because I follow what the judge wants. I become inmate of the year and am rewarded by a trip to the jail in Washington D.C. where I get to listen to guest speakers talk about their role in helping people stay out of trouble in the jail. There, I am also able to meet with several staffers who give me good advice to stay away from a life of crime.

💰

It's eight years later, and I'm at the toilet paper factory where my brother works. My living room is ten by twelve feet with a computer, a thirty-two-inch flat screen TV, and overstuffed furniture. I'm happy that my life is straight, and I am still receiving counseling.

ACKNOWLEDGMENTS

There are many people I would like to thank, but if I start giving names, other names could be left out. The influences are sixteen years in vending, outlook Nebraska Inc., along with reading books and old-time radio programs for which I'm grateful.

ABOUT THE AUTHOR

Anthony Scott Engle was born to Shirley Engle, and his father is unknown. Shirley was married three times before her death in 1992. Anthony was raised mostly in Peoria, Illinois. His current job is with Outlook Nebraska, Inc., and he is a former employee of the year. His previous job was The Business Enterprise for the Blind for sixteen years. Anthony is married and has four step-children. He also has several grand-children and three great grand-children.

www.ingramcontent.com/pod-product-compliance
Lightning Source LLC
Chambersburg PA
CBHW021920170626
46807CB00007B/2914